WITHDRAWN

Large Print Way
Way, Margaret.
Strategy for marriage

STACKS

STRATEGY FOR MARRIAGE

STRATEGY FOR MARRIAGE

BY

MARGARET WAY

MILLS & BOON®

*MILLS & BOON and
MILLS & BOON with the Rose Device
are registered trademarks of the publisher.*

*First published in Great Britain 2002
Large Print edition 2002
Harlequin Mills & Boon Limited,
Eton House, 18-24 Paradise Road,
Richmond, Surrey TW9 1SR*

© *Margaret Way, Pty., Ltd 2002*

ISBN 0 263 17372 0

*Set in Times Roman 16½ on 17½ pt.
16-1102-50608*

*Printed and bound in Great Britain
by Antony Rowe Ltd, Chippenham, Wiltshire*

CHAPTER ONE

*Deakin-McKinnon Wedding
Reception—McKinnon Riverside Mansion
Brisbane, Queensland*

"Ashe, darling, who is that girl?'' The blonde in the exquisite green dress?'' Mercedes, his aunt by marriage and mother of the bride, dug him in the ribs, a worried frown on her brow.

"You mean Ms. Botticelli?'' His answer, even to his ears, was sardonic. "I've been wondering the same thing.'' In fact he'd begun to marvel at just the amount of attention he was giving that particular young woman and was amazed at the unprecedented thrust of sexual desire she aroused in him. He'd grown cynical, really cynical, about a woman's beauty and her ability to hold a man spellbound. Beautiful women in the style of this blonde reminded him of his runaway mother. The mother he'd hated and ached for since she'd abandoned him and his father when he was ten years old.

"No one on our side seems to know her," Mercedes whispered with genuine concern, her fingers fidgeting with her extremely valuable string of 19 mm Australian South Sea pearls, the finest in the world. "That is to say everyone I've asked. Oh for heaven's sake why am I worried?" She gave a false little laugh. "It's not as though she isn't beautiful and well behaved but I mean it's fairly obvious our dear Josh seems to know her even if he's not going anywhere near her. Would you mind awfully, darling, getting some idea of who exactly she is?"

The fact was he'd been about to make his move. For one thing "our dear Josh" was the bridegroom. A possible ex-girlfriend didn't help. "No problem, Mercedes." He smiled down at her. "Leave it to me." He was extremely fond of Mercedes, and his quiet little cousin, Callista, who looked as radiant as she could ever look on this day of days. Sad to say he hadn't taken to her new husband, Josh Deakin. In his most suspicious moments, which were frequent, he was a suspicious person, he thought Deakin the male equivalent of the proverbial gold-digger. At one time he'd very nearly said so, worried Deakin was only after Callista's money. The problem was Mercedes was very taken with him and Callista was clearly head over heels in love. She wouldn't have listened. She'd have dug in her heels. Although Callista dearly loved her mother, at twenty-nine she was anxious to escape the nest, get married and set up her own home. This was a fairytale wedding he'd been told. Who believed in fairytales? Certainly not him, though he had to admit Ms. Botticelli looked magical.

Mercedes' rich contralto brought him out of his reverie. "Everything is going marvellously," she said as though at any moment all could change. "The last thing we need is for something—um-um—" She stared across the crowded room at the beautiful blonde, seeking the right word.

"Don't fret. I told you I'd handle it," he soothed, hoping to God it wasn't already all too late. But if Deakin imagined Mercedes and Callista didn't have someone looking out for them, he'd better think again.

"You're my great support, Ashe," Mercedes told him fondly. "I'm afraid I lean on you for so much."

"We're family, Mercedes," he offered lightly when he didn't feel lightly about family at all. He was head of a clan even if his immediate family had gone. His mother with her lover. They lived mostly in New York. His father and his uncle Sholto, Mercedes' late husband, had been killed in a light plane crash five years ago. An event that made some people say the family was cursed. Maybe it was. It had had its fair share of tragedies. So in his late twenties he had become head of the family, head of the McKinnon pastoral empire, executor of the Family Trust. He took his responsibilities very seriously.

As Mercedes, in a very becoming silvery outfit, sailed off towards her guests he acknowledged he hadn't told her he'd had his eye on Ms. Botticelli since she'd gatecrashed the reception. His well-honed instincts warned him that was the case but he didn't want to put a blight on such a day by overreacting. He'd take his time. She'd done it in the cheekiest way possible. Two ushers were guarding the open double doors of the McKinnon mansion taking the wedding invitations from the guests and checking them against their lists when he spotted her arrival from the head of the gallery.

He couldn't look away. He who was very good at taking a woman's beauty and aura in his stride. She was tall, even taller in high-heeled sandals. She wore a ravishingly pretty dress, a froth of chiffon, printed in a swirl of different greens. The crossover sleeveless bodice showed a tantalising glimpse of the curves of her breasts, the short ruffled skirt sprinkled with glittering little beads showed off her lovely long legs. High up on one shoulder was a huge rose made out of the same material sprinkled with brilliants like the skirt. It was an outfit only a beautiful young woman with a perfect figure and lots of self-confidence could wear without risking the dress overwhelming her.

So there she was. A long-stemmed mystery blonde, her hair drawn back from her face into a high knot, the rest of her mane cascading down her back to past her shoulder blades. The overhead chandelier, plus the last rays of sunshine, washed her in light, so she gave off a spectacular sparkle. Her skin, he could see clearly, was a smooth textured cream, blushed over the high cheekbones. There was a shallow cleft in her chin; her eyes even at this distance were a clear light green set at a faint slant as were her darkened brows. She looked excited, a beautiful young thing who inexplicably had no partner, so why did he get the odd feeling all the animation didn't spell happy. Far from it. More like nerve-ridden. He moved further down the staircase feeling another hot surge of desire. It made him irrationally hostile even as it served to remind him he was human.

Who was she exactly? How did she fit in? He thought he knew all of Callista's friends. God knows she and Mercedes had tried to match him up to quite a few, not even listening when he warned them off. He saw her make a little play of rummaging in her glittery purse for her invitation—but then she saw across the marble floored atrium someone she knew. Her face broke into a lovely infectious smile and she waved, calling a name. Instantly, tactfully, the ushers let the beautiful creature go in. Women like that were unmistakably Somebody. Anyone could see that. As a bit of play-acting it was darn near perfect.

Just as he suspected, she didn't head towards anyone in particular. There was no one waiting for her. She walked right on, flashing iridescent glances around the elegant entrance hall massed with flowers. She hadn't been at the church. No way he would have missed her. But she'd turned up at the reception. Interesting! It wasn't a sit-down affair where guests were allotted seats at a table. That might have proved a mite difficult even for an enterprising young woman. Instead a sumptuous buffet had been arranged. It was to be served from the huge bridal marquees that had been erected in the three-acre garden. The dessert table alone Mercedes had told him was one hundred foot long. Mercedes had spared no expense to make this a great day for her only child.

Now they had a gatecrasher. Albeit a woman whose beauty had made the breath catch in his throat. That alone made him laugh and his laugh was deep with self-mockery. In his action-packed life he had no time for a woman who could keep a man in thrall. He had too much on his mind. Too much to do. This woman was Trouble. Moreover she was somehow connected to Josh Deakin, his cousin's bridegroom of only a few hours. The ex-girlfriend immediately sprang to mind. An ex-girlfriend perhaps bent on some kind of disruption. No way! He had the sure feeling at some point he would have to hustle Ms.

Botticelli out of the house. And that was quite a while before Mercedes had put voice to her own niggling concerns.

Christy, sick with nerves but too angry and upset to abort her mission, made it through the front door of the two-story McKinnon mansion. Her nerve was holding. It was a shocking breach of etiquette to gatecrash a wedding. On so many levels she deeply regretted it, but her ex-boyfriend, Josh, the man who had convinced her he loved her, deserved a good fright. She had no intention whatsoever of upsetting the bride, the McKinnon heiress. The bride was probably a young woman as gullible as herself. Josh, after all, was all charm on the surface. The only difference between her and the bride was around 15 million, not to mention what that fortunate young woman would eventually inherit from her mother, Mrs. Mercedes McKinnon, a woman of considerable substance and the widow of the late Sholto McKinnon, well-known pastoralist and philanthropist. While Josh had been courting his heiress, he'd also continued his ardent courtship of her. How many times had he told her he loved her? How many times had he brought up the subject of marriage? She'd seriously been considering entering into an engagement. Six months of having a lovely time together. *Fun* really. In retrospect no depth. It all came to a halt when by sheer chance she saw Josh kissing another woman outside the very law courts that figured so often in his fund of amusing stories. Josh was an up-and-coming lawyer. The young woman turned out to be today's bride, Callista McKinnon, now Mrs. Josh Deakin. Even as Josh had been proclaiming his love for her, he'd been courting the heiress. Fate had played its hand. Mrs. Mercedes McKinnon, a favoured client of the prestigious law firm where Josh worked as an associate, came into the offices one day bringing her petite, pretty daughter, Callista. Josh was especially good with female clients so his boss allowed him in on proceedings. It had to be that very day Josh realized a golden opportunity had opened up for him. With a rich wife the world was his oyster. Josh was very ambitious. Money was important to him. *Real money*. Social position. Obviously he saw an instant rocketing up the ladder. She had never fully understood that side of Josh. Not that she had really known him at all. He was a liar for one. A traitor. A good actor who could excel in any number of parts. The very worst aspect was as he told her about his plans to marry Callista he spoke like a man who had come into a huge lottery win. A win they were *both* going to share. She'd have died before accepting that shocking lack of integrity. Josh Deakin, cad that he was, had earned himself this lesson. But she still couldn't stop her nerves crackling.

Halfway across the gracious entrance hall, a perfect setting for valuable antiques and magnificent arrangements of fresh flowers, she became aware she was under close surveillance. She couldn't fail to know by now her blond good looks attracted attention but the gaze that was concentrated on her didn't send out any currents of admiration. It felt more like she was under an extremely daunting inspection. And found suspect. Her senses were so wired she was drawn to look upwards, searching out the origin of that magnetic beam.

Her green eyes widened in shock. Her gaze honed in a man standing at the curve of the elegant staircase, looking down at her with brilliant near-black eyes.

Ashe McKinnon.

It took her less than an instant to recognise him. He was even more damn-your-eyes handsome and arrogant than his photographs. After Josh had told her of his plan to marry into the McKinnon clan, she had felt upset enough to make it her business to find out what she could about them. And there was plenty. They were a pioneering dynasty. Cattle kings from colonial times who had generated great wealth. She'd seen photographs of the current McKinnon and his ancestral home in Channel Country South West Queensland. It was a magnificent homestead. There were photographs of him at different functions, including a brilliant action shot of him playing polo, arm thrown back for a full free swing. She'd know him anywhere. In fact the sight of him gave her the oddest sick thrill. He didn't look a kind man. Far from it. He looked formidable. Certainly not the sort of man who'd tolerate having a gatecrasher at his cousin's wedding.

Christy moved swiftly. All she wanted was the opportunity, however brief, to give Josh the fright of his life. The most she intended was to give him a little wave. Then she'd go home happy, or as happy as a girl could be when a man had humiliated her. She hadn't

written Ashe McKinnon into the scenario at
all. A huge mistake. She had the shivery feeling he could catch up with her very soon.
Christy made her way into the opulent living
room, impressed despite herself at the decor
and the magnificent artworks on the walls.

"A friend of the groom?" an attractive
voice queried at her ear. She spun on her high
heels relieved beyond words to see a tall red-
haired young man beaming down at her, his
bright blue eyes filled with the sort of admiring
look she was used to.

She was safe for a while. She intended to
stay until she had her little moment of revenge
on Josh, and Ashe McKinnon, the big cattle
baron, could go to hell.

Of course she had no difficulty easing herself
in. Not with that intoxicating image. From the
open glass doorway leading into the plant-
filled solarium Ashe watched her, openly marvelling at her audacity. He saw all the bache-
lors in sight make their moves on her. He
couldn't believe his response. It angered him.
He wanted to tell Jake Reid, a guy he'd known
all his life, to take his big hands off her. Even

the muscles in his shoulders tensed. This was so unlike him.

The solarium had been turned into a ball-room. Lots of couples had taken the floor to a plethora of styles that ranged from old-fashioned elegance to near gallops. He waited his moment, subtly keeping an eye on her, then he excused himself from the group around him.

"Pardon me." He tapped his friend, Tim Westbury, on the shoulder. "I really ought to introduce myself to your partner."

"Heck, Ashe, we were having such a good time."

For a moment it looked like Tim was going to hang in there until he saw his expression.

"So I noticed. Goodbye, Tim."

"Catch you later, Christy," Tim called before he was swept away by his current girl-friend who eyed "Christy" balefully.

"Wonderful party." He put his arm around her, a strange pleasure, and inhaled her fragrance, freesias spiked with something citrus.

"Wonderful," she agreed, turning her face away, all poise when her heart was thumping with fright.

"Beautiful wedding ceremony."

"It brought tears to my eyes."

"Truly?"

"I never lie."

"Perhaps you have on this occasion. I had the notion you weren't at the church at all. Ashe McKinnon, by the way. I'm Callista's cousin."

She frowned slightly, her eyes as green as peridots. "You don't look in the least alike." It was hard not to be impressed by him. Aesthetically anyway. How best to describe him? All commanding male. A touch severe. Yet the kind of man women went wild over. Not her. She already knew he was too tough for her, but he did look wonderful in his formal morning suit, traditional grey with a very dashing burgundy silk cravat.

She knew from her partner, Tim, he had given the bride away. Head of the family and all that. He certainly looked the part. His height alone made him stand out. He was well over six feet, but lean, powerful. He made her feel small and at five-eight she was tall for a woman. She could feel the whipcord musculature in his arms and along his back. He was very strong.

Christy continued her abstract inspection. A deep permanent tan, not Josh's beach boy stuff, Ashe's was trademark Outback. He had lustrous black hair with a natural wave. If he let it grow a centimetre longer it would spring into curls. His eyes were really beautiful, brilliant like glittering whirlpools. She couldn't see into them but he seemed to be looking right through her.

He wasn't a sweet man. Or a man who would make a woman feel safe. He looked dangerous enough to be treated with caution. There was so much tension there. A hard impatience that was communicating itself to her. Then again he possessed a stand-apart elegance, very much in keeping with a glamorous member of the landed elite. No question about his pedigree. And he just *knew* about her. So what was he going to do, throw her out? For all he knew she could put up a struggle. Or maybe he had taken her measure. There was only one person she intended to embarrass and that was Josh.

He received her long scrutiny, totally unfazed. "I'm dying to know your name," he prompted, dark voice sardonic.

"You have only to ask me. Christine Parker. My friends call me Christy."

Her answer was gentle and low. Music. Another ace up her sleeve.

"Then I'll call you Miss Parker. Are you a friend of the bridegroom, may I ask?" He slid his hand along her back with the surety she had a beautiful supple body.

"Now why does that sound like you've thrown out a challenge?" she parried.

"Possibly because you're the sort of woman who responds to one."

"I mean no harm, Mr. McKinnon. I want you to understand that."

"I'm pleased to hear it." He gave her a sardonic glance. "I can't have you spoiling my cousin's day."

"I have no intention of doing anything like that," she protested. "There's no spite in my nature."

"But you're looking to upset Deakin?"

"Now you sound like you don't care." It was wonderful to be able to challenge him. There was something very dangerous about being close to this man. It gave her quite a jolt. In her altered state she compared it to shock therapy. Something was happening to her. She didn't know what.

"My only concern is this reception goes off beautifully," he said in a warning voice that left her flushed. "I'm devoted to my aunt and cousin."

"Really?" All of a sudden Christy needed to lash out, her anger and humiliation festering. "From the look of you I wouldn't have thought you had a tender bone in your body."

"Play it cool, Miss Parker," he said.

There was considerable heat between them. Christy realised with a sense of astonishment a lot of it was sexual. She wondered how that could possibly be when she still considered herself jilted by Josh. She could feel the imprint of this man's hand right through the chiffon of her dress. It might have been pressed against her naked flesh. Her perceptions so long blunted by acute dismay were now razor-sharp. But then he was a striking, powerful, physical man, she reasoned, quite without the easy-going gentleness with which Josh had surrounded her.

Looking down at her telltale face, his expression tautened. "Let's go," he said abruptly. The tips of her breasts were giving him little shocks as they brushed up against him.

"Where?" She threw up her head, startled. His face was quite unreadable.

"Out into the garden," he suggested curtly. "All the time we've been dancing Deakin has been staring over here. Even with his bride on his arm."

"Pay no attention," she said. But she hoped Josh was staring. He looked so deeply familiar she thought she couldn't bear the whole situation. Callista looked so nice. She deserved to be happy. Christy's instinct told her it wouldn't be for long. Not with Josh. Josh wasn't good enough. Josh's only real fondness was for money. But Callista on her big day looked radiant in her beautiful ecru satin gown that glimmered with thousands of seed pearls. Her billowy floor-length organza veil was held off her small face by an exquisite diamond-and-pearl diadem that looked like a family heirloom.

After all that she knew, Christy still wished perversely things could have been different. That Josh could have been different from the man he really was.

"How well did you know him?" Ashe McKinnon asked her, his dark face taking on an aspect of contempt.

"I don't think you want to listen."

"Try me," he clipped off.

"It's all in the past. Another dimension." She needed a huge breathing space from this man.

"It'd better be." With one hand he lifted her face and turned his black gaze on her.

"What do you want to do, crush me?" She envied him his masculine strength. The hard detachment.

Instantly he eased his grip. What did he want with her? To pick her up and carry her off? To make love to her until she couldn't even remember who Deakin was?

"Are you suggesting I could be *that* physical?"

"I could feel your anger." Yet something about him was giving her a deep, languorous feeling. It was like being engulfed in the black velvet of night. What was she doing twisting and turning in this stranger's arms? He was so totally different from Josh. With a powerful magnetism that reached through her pain.

Moreover he was controlling her, pulling her closer.

"So are you going to tell me exactly why you are here? I'm certain you have no invitation."

"I let it get away from me." She glanced at him briefly, her lashes shadowing her eyes. "It flew into the air and blew away." There was no comfort in this man, only astonishing heat. She kept seeing Josh and his bride out of the corner of her eye. Hurt spasmed through her. "Kiss me," she ordered before she started to cry.

He shook her a little. "Because you want to make him jealous? Look at me." He was going to kiss her before the night was over. He had never wanted to kiss a woman more in his life. This beautiful creature who was electric for another man. A man who had his cousin lovingly tucked into his shoulder. "You little fool," Ashe muttered, lowering his dark head protectively over her. "There's no way, no way, you can get him back."

"I don't want him back. I don't!" She knew it was true but she couldn't get herself together almost overnight.

"Is that a prayer?"

Her mouth was trembling beneath his brooding regard. "Could we go outside?"

"Why not? We're leaving a lot of burning curiosity behind."

It was not to be. Callista called to her cousin from across the room.

"Ashe!" No one had told Callista who the beautiful blond girl in the green dress was. She was extravagantly lovely to Callista's eyes. The dress! She could never wear a dress like that. And Ashe? What was he doing with her? The two of them looked somehow torched. As if no one else in the world mattered.

Beside Callista, Josh gave a wry little exclamation. "What with all this talking I'm getting dry in the throat. I think I'll get myself a drink. Could I get you anything, my darling?"

Callista gave him her sweet smile. "Oh, Joshua, please stay and meet Ashe's new girlfriend. I must say I'm surprised. But then Ashe is the best of anyone at surprises."

"I don't know…" Josh's mouth was indeed dry and his heart was thundering. Christy was always such a lady but he knew what angry women could do.

"Please, darling, for me." Callista caught her bridegroom's hand.

"I can't do this," Christy confessed to Ashe McKinnon as they crossed the floor.

"You can. I'll see you through." He took her hand and held it firmly.

"Who am I?" This wasn't what she intended at all. "Who am I supposed to be?"

"You should have thought of that." His reply was a little harsh. "You're my deepest secret."

"You mean *you* asked me?" She was drowning in confusion.

"Who else? I'm not going to risk Callista's being badly hurt. Do you think you can smile?" He eyed her critically.

"Of course I can smile, you arrogant man." A storm of outraged pride blew up in her. He had calluses on his palm. McKinnon the cattle baron. High power—high voltage. She had an hysterical desire to run from him.

"Would you just look at Deakin?" he said suddenly in a hard gritty voice. "My bet is he was trying to make a break for it but Callista stopped him."

Even devastated by Josh's betrayal, Christy could scarcely blame him.

"So what's the play?" she asked through small clenched teeth. It was almost as though she'd known this man in another life, but she had no time to dwell on that.

"We'll play it by ear," he told her, giving her, quite out the blue, the sexiest smile.

It was so amazing it put the adrenalin back into her.

And hey! Josh had the frozen look of a rabbit caught in a hunter's sights. Callista, the triumphant bride, was looking from her to her cousin as if she didn't know what was going on. Up close Christy realised Callista was older than she had supposed. Late rather than early twenties. Probably her trust fund paid out at age thirty. The evidence was Josh couldn't wait.

"You look absolutely lovely and so happy, Callista," Ashe told his cousin in a surprisingly calm voice. "I hope nothing ever changes that." He slid his arm smoothly around Christy's waist, drawing her forward. "I'd like you to meet a friend of mine, Christy Parker. She wasn't on the guest list because I didn't know she'd be back from L.A."

Josh, aware he had escaped some terrible danger, fell into his role of loving bridegroom, the expression on his face growing in confidence. "We know one another, don't we?" he asked Christy, quite unforgivably, giving Christy a smile for which one really needed sunglasses. ''You're with Whitelaw Promotions, aren't you?''

It was her moment to bring him down. To give him instant payback. Instead she nodded coolly. ''That's right. I think I know you, too.''

Josh prepared himself again for an on-slaught. It didn't come. ''So tell me, how is Zack?'' he asked in the nicest friendly fashion. He referred to Christy's boss and the head of the public relations company.

''Fine.'' She couldn't possibly slip into casual mode. She was far too upset. ''It's been a beautiful wedding, Callista.'' She turned her attention to the bride. ''I wish you every happiness.'' Amazingly she was able to say it.

''Thank you so much…Christy…'' Callista finally got her voice going. ''Wherever did you meet Ashe?'' She looked avid to know.

''Well…''

''It's a long story,'' Ashe McKinnon said, locking Christy of the shining beauty to him, aware of her turmoil. She was as jumpy as a cat.

"A story worth listening to, I'll bet." Josh's glance lingered long on Christy.

"Christy's not talking." Ashe's vibrant voice was saturated in what sounded very much like sarcasm. "See you later, you two. I know how much you both want to be together."

"Dear God!" Christy murmured almost inaudibly as they moved off. "I don't normally drink but I feel like one now."

"You did very well," he assured her. "It was plain to me you wanted to slap him."

"Whereas *you* didn't?" Whatever this man said, he fired her. "I thought you came dangerously near to cutting."

"I'm surprised you said that," he drawled. "But then you don't know me. If I'd been really cutting Deakin wouldn't be standing. 'Don't I know you'?" He aped Josh's lighter tones then they hardened. "Only the fact Callista is my cousin and she's wearing a wedding dress stopped me from asking him to step outside."

"I can't imagine he could stand up to your flailing fists." She shuddered. Josh would be no match for this cattle baron. He didn't have that sort of invincible masculinity. In fact, she considered very belatedly, Josh was *soft*.

"My dear girl, I'd drop him in one." He signalled to one of the fleet of uniformed waiters who hurried to his side. "Thank you," he said gracefully, taking two glasses of champagne from the silver tray.

"I should go now," Christy said quite sadly as he passed a flute to her.

"My dear, you should be thrown out," Ashe quipped, not liking this beautiful witch's misery.

"I don't belong here."

"I entirely agree with you, but you're not going anywhere. Not yet. Come." He took her arm. Held her captive. "Let's leave all these good people to their exuberant high spirits. I expect you're hungry?"

"No." She shook her head, fighting for her dignity.

"I promise you you will be. Enough money has been spent on the food and drink at this reception to feed the entire Outback for a year."

As they made their way out to the marquee society photographers got in the way. Flashes went off, capturing the two of them strolling along like a pair of lovers. Ashe McKinnon didn't stop to supply Christy's name. He didn't have to, Christy thought shakily. At least one photographer knew exactly who she was since he'd photographed her at various functions a few times before. Without question a photograph of her with Ashe McKinnon at her side would appear in *Vogue*, or whatever magazine had the rights. No matter what, Christy held her shoulders back and her head high.

The food was indeed so sumptuous many of the guests stood gawking in awe before they finally moved in to sample the endless dishes. Ice sculptures in the form of larger-than-life swans decorated the tables, which were festooned with white flowers and trails of ivy down the centre. Billows of white tulle and satin ribbons decorated the tented ceilings with thousands of fresh white flowers including masses of white orchids flown in from Thailand. Christy had already seen the six-foot-high wedding cake, which dominated the twenty-foot-long Georgian dining room table. Obviously the happy couple were to cut the cake in the house. She hoped to be long gone by then. Why hadn't the cattle baron thrown her out? He was a strange perverse man.

Instead he made her eat something. "Go on," he urged. "Everyone is looking at you. Isn't that too priceless? Of course you're the most beautiful woman here, though I expect you still want to change places with Callista?"

She was aghast at his little cruelties. "What a pig you are. *Cochon!*"

"But of course you speak French," he joked. "Anyway I'll pretend I didn't hear that." He bent his glistening dark head over hers, a study in ebony and gold, as though he was whispering endearments.

"No need to overdo it," she said sharply, struck again by the beauty of his eyes. Why did men have such wonderful eyelashes?

"I'm doing what I want to do. It's even possible I've fallen madly in love with you."

"And pray have you?" She could barely conceal her inner rage.

"No. We're co-conspirators that's all. And I'm damned if I know why. Our paths will probably never cross again."

"Amen to that," she flashed. This wasn't a man you sashayed around. He was a big, powerful tough man. The sort of man she disliked.

"You don't see me as eligible?" he mocked. "They tell me I am."

"Why not with all that money," she returned bleakly. Wasn't that how it went with Josh.

"You have such command of diplomacy. I'm sure you weren't always that cynical."

"I was not." There was a headache behind her eyes.

"You're thinking about Deakin, aren't you?" he abruptly accused, the muscles of his face tautening.

"It's hard not to when I've turned up at his wedding," she managed painfully.

"And when did you decide to do that?" He was determined to know.

"At precisely half past eleven last night," she replied.

"What we call a snap decision? More champagne? There's a choice. Moet or Bollinger?"

"Wouldn't it have been cheaper, even smarter, to buy domestic?" she asked tartly, swallowing a morsel of Russian caviar.

"Mercedes thinks our champagne styles lack French subtlety."

"She should go to more wine tastings. Even the experts have been known to be fooled."

Inevitably other guests surged up to speak to Ashe. He appeared to be known and "adored" by everyone on the bride's side, but needless to say none of the super-rich knew her. She only occasionally moved into their world at charity functions. But he introduced her to all his friends who turned searching but approving eyes on her. It was about time Ashe got married, they said with sly glances at her, never guessing she was wincing inside. As urbanely as Ashe McKinnon was handling all this, she just knew there was a dark side to the cattle baron. He was allowing this charade to go on to prevent a scandal. She was determined to get away from him, at the same time filled with the weird notion she couldn't even if she tried. But her moment came. The best-looking of the bridesmaids, four in all, all dressed alike in shades of blue moire silk, determinedly took hold of his arm.

"Ashe, darling, why are you being so cruel to me…?"

Christy waited for no more. She fled across the lawn, keeping to the shadows and away from the main reception rooms, heading eastwards. If she got lost he would have to send a search party. She'd have really strange memories of all this. They'd probably stay with her all her life.

Just when she thought she was safe, a man's hand suddenly reached for her, drawing her back into a large dimly lit room that looked like a man's study. She had an impression of walls of books, glass cases bearing sporting trophies, paintings of winning racehorses, a desk and chairs.

"Christy!" Josh was staring down at her, soft floppy hair nearly falling into his eyes.

"Sorry, sorry, sorry, I don't want to speak to you." She gritted her teeth.

"Take it quietly, darling," he begged. "God, I thought the bloody cattle baron had abducted you."

"He'll be coming to look for me pretty soon," Christy warned, wanting nothing more than to have Ashe McKinnon explode into the room.

"You *don't* know him, do you?" Josh asked as if he guessed her pitiful secret.

"Pretty soon we're going to get engaged," Christy said briskly, wanting to see how he took it.

The generous mouth dropped open. "Be serious."

"I am being serious," she managed.

"You're not!" Now he gloated. "You don't know him. He doesn't come to the city that often. He has a cattle empire to run."

"I know!" Christy flaunted the knowledge. "He's very rich."

"You don't care about riches."

"I do now. It's ironic, isn't it? I'd say he has even more millions than your wife and mother-in-law put together."

"You're bitter, aren't you?" Josh accused her, his hazel eyes raking her face and body.

"Get a grip, Josh," she said, green eyes narrowing in contempt. "It's okay you married your Callista. There's a big wide world out there full of gorgeous men. Ashe McKinnon would have to be right up there at the top."

"You weren't on the wedding list," Josh pointed out aggressively. "You're a fake, Christy. You don't know him at all." But on his own wedding day Josh's voice cracked with jealousy.

"How would you know?" Christy was finding his behaviour abominable. "It's been weeks since I laid eyes on you. Now if you don't mind I want to leave."

"When you're McKinnon's date?" He challenged her to stop.

"I mean leave this room. You have me bailed up." She stared at him in disgust, willing him out of the way.

"No one will come in here, Christy," he said as if to reassure her.

"Oh, please. You'd better hope and pray not Ashe McKinnon. You could wind up dead. He's very protective of his cousin."

"I can handle Callista." He smiled tightly. "I had to talk to you, Christy. I have to see you later."

"Later?" Her eyes flashed angrily even while her voice rose in sheer disbelief. "Later you're supposed to be on your honeymoon. Not renewing our relationship."

"How I wish it was you," he admitted in a tone of deepest regret.

"Go to hell." She prised her fingers from his arm. "And I hope you stay there."

"Why are you doing this to me?" he groaned, his eyes curiously glazed. "I love you. You love me. Nothing can change that." He reached, as though this time she would surrender and go into his arms.

Instead the tall, powerful figure of Ashe McKinnon appeared in the open doorway. He fairly lunged into the room, looking as daunting as the devil, just as dangerous, and probably just as unlawful.

"This has to be the most stupid thing you've ever done, Deakin," he rasped, eyes like black diamonds. "Get away from him." He turned on Christy, grinding out the order.

Giving orders was a tendency in dangerous creatures, she thought, instantly obeying.

"Hasn't it crossed your arrogant mind that's what I'm trying to do?" The decided edge in her voice matched his own.

"I told you to stay with me," he reminded her, not taking his eyes off the errant bridegroom who had taken cover of sorts behind an armchair.

"And you really thought I was going to obey? What sort of woman do you think I am?" Christy fired, embarrassed beyond words.

"An idiot to begin with," he informed her shortly. "Come over here to me."

She knew better than to rile him further.

"What are we going to do with you, Deakin?" Ashe felt like slamming Callista's brand-new husband against a wall. "My family is very important to me." And in all honesty he was seething at the sight of Miss Parker near wrapped in Deakin's arms.

"It wasn't what you think." The panic-stricken Josh assumed a look of deep apology. Tangling with the cattle baron would be like tangling with a charging rhino. "It's the same old story. You must know it, Ashe." His mobile features took on a man-to-man expression. "Christy and I had a little fling but when I told her it was over she wouldn't let go. Women are like that."

She had never known this man, Christy thought, gazing at him with a mixture of dismay and pain.

"You really think I'm going to swallow that?" Ashe near choked, he was so angry. He couldn't, absolutely couldn't, relate to this guy. What in the name of God did Callista and this girl, Christy, see in him? He was ninety-five per cent toxic waste.

"It's true." Christy picked that moment to be utterly selfless. Not for Josh. Sometime in the future Josh would get his comeuppance. But for Callista. She had no desire to hurt Callista. Callista was just another woman who thought herself deeply in love with a man she couldn't see clearly. "I came here to tempt him."

"What rot!" Ashe bridled afresh. "About as good as it gets." He studied Christy with contemptuous eyes. "You're trying to save his worthless skin."

"Your cousin Callista doesn't deserve this. She's the innocent party. I owe her something. The question I ask myself now is why did *you*, astute old *you*, let her marry him?"

Ashe's dynamic face mirrored his frustration. "The fact is Callista is nearly thirty years old." He rounded on Christy, his anger abruptly abating when he saw how pale she was. Her eyes were enormous, a dead give-away she was deeply disturbed.

"Get the hell out of here, Deakin," Ashe ordered, his voice cracking like a whip. "Your playing around with other women ends today. If I hear one word…!"

"I'm going to be the best husband ever," Josh proclaimed like a professional con man, looking Ashe in the eyes.

"You'd better be, my man." Ashe nodded, his expression grim.

"I love Callista," Josh poured it on while Ashe McKinnon threw back his dark head and roared.

"I have grave misgivings about that. You're dirt."

The rest of Josh's words dried up. Hastily he crossed to the door, pausing a moment from its relative safety. "As far as I'm concerned Christy is the culprit here. Ex-girlfriends aren't supposed to gatecrash a man's wedding."

Ashe swore beneath his breath in a near ecstasy of anger. "Get out of here." The attitude of his body suggesting a panther about to spring into action.

Josh wasn't entirely insane. With one last aggrieved look he took to his heels.

"Not his finest hour," pronounced Ashe in disgust.

When the time came—by now time had no meaning for Christy—for the happy couple to leave on the first leg of their honeymoon—an overnight stay in the honeymoon suite of a leading hotel before jetting off for three weeks in Thailand—the guests had assembled on the grand sweep of front lawn of the McKinnon mansion to wave them off.

Callista, as pretty as a picture in her pink going-away outfit, turned to throw her bouquet. A surprisingly high sweep. Christy, battling with the illusion she was trapped in a dream, made no move to catch it. She felt quite naturally it was inappropriate as well as the fact she had gone off weddings. She didn't even make a playful gesture of reaching up as all four bridesmaids were doing, but in earnest. The bouquet simply descending gracefully but in a mesmerizing way, twirling and twirling a lovely posy of perfect pink and white roses threaded with traceries of green.

The bridesmaids were running forward, palms up, fingers steepled, each one determined to catch this wonderful forecast. I'm next! Their faces were bright with excitement and anticipatory pleasure.

Me. Me. Let it be me.

But life is full of disappointments and pre-ordained events. Callista's bouquet fell with a soft fragrant weight into Christy's nerveless hands.

She saw the muscles along Ashe McKinnon's clean-cut jaw tighten cynically before two of the women guests grasped her in affectionate camaraderie and kissed her on either cheek.

"Lucky girl!" They batted speculative glances at Ashe. God, wasn't he a drop-dead hunk!

And why not? Ashe had scarcely left her side. Mercedes had berated him fondly for trying to fool her. Everyone seemed to think she was the new woman in Ashe McKinnon's life. An irony not lost on either of them.

And so it was that Christy and Ashe McKinnon left the wedding together. Christy heading into very deep waters indeed.

CHAPTER TWO

FROM nowhere a chauffeured limousine appeared. At least there were some pluses to being rich. Christy stepped into the back seat. After a moment Ashe McKinnon joined her.

In the silence that followed, Christy stared out the window, devastated by the whole day.

"Silly me, I've forgotten where you live," he said in an ironic tone.

She surveyed him gravely, her faith in life shattered, yet it was he who had rescued her from a very bad situation.

"Goodness me, and you were thinking of moving in. Number 10 Downing Street." At least that was a world away.

"My dear girl they've changed the locks." His black gaze fell on her lovely face, desire lapping in his blood.

"Then I suggest you try 121 Shelly Beach Road."

He lowered the partition window to give instructions to the chauffeur.

"I feel ashamed of myself," Christy confessed after a few unhappy minutes of studying the stars. "Really ashamed."

"Perhaps you ought to be put in prison," he suggested in a mocking voice.

"It wasn't that serious, was it?" She looked back at him. Why was she with this man?

"You do this for a living, gatecrashing receptions?"

"I couldn't face seeing Josh marry your cousin. How petite she is! Doll-size."

"Up until recently I thought she had a woman-sized brain. As for you, you have to get on with your life." He didn't want her mourning Deakin. Not for one minute.

"I don't want to even think about it for at least forty-eight hours. I had maybe one too many glasses of champagne," she apologised.

"That's perfectly understandable. It's also the reason why I hired the limousine. I couldn't drive you myself. Not only do I not keep a car in the city but I'm well over the limit. Three glasses of anything is surely not enough to celebrate a wedding? Even an insufferable one."

"I should have known better." Christy gave a bruised sigh.

"Indeed you should." His tone used up a lot of censure.

"You've never made a mistake in your life I suppose?" Christy pressed back exhaustedly against the plush upholstery.

"I think I hate the way you say that. All my ex-girlfriends speak to me."

"I bet you gave them a hard time," Christy answered. He wouldn't lie to them. If anything he was too much up-front. "I know some women go in for excitement and danger. It must make them feel more alive. It's my professional judgment that you're a dangerous man."

"All it might take is a little getting to know me." He flung out an arm and drew her close to him. His desire for her was blocking out his usual tight control. And he wanted to comfort her. All of a sudden she seemed very vulnerable.

Christy allowed her head to come to rest against his shoulder. "You know you're not my keeper." But he was *very* masterful.

"I am for this evening." He brushed a few glinting golden strands of hair from her cheek. "To be honest, I'm concerned you might go after them."

She came upright in despair. "I've learned my lesson."

"I sincerely hope so." He didn't sound impressed. "Your ex-boyfriend and my cousin have only this very evening exchanged their marriage vows."

"And good luck to them," Christy exclaimed disjointedly. She felt so overwrought she couldn't even begin to describe her emotions. "I do know one thing. I wouldn't want to marry a man like you." She withdrew the ruffled hem of her short skirt away from his trousered knee.

"I hope you weren't counting on my asking you?" He didn't bother to control the mockery. Who the hell did she think she was? A goddess?

"Getting married is the last thing I want to do," Christy said with the sombre gravity of the betrayed. "Marriages in most cases don't seem to work out. I know any number of couples who have split up."

"Not counting you and Josh?" He smiled grimly.

"When I think of you a word comes to mind," Christy said in exasperation. Didn't he know she was badly hurt?

"Please don't say it," he joked. "I detest hearing rough words on a woman's tongue. As it happens, I'm not a great one for marriage either. It's something men have to do to get heirs."

She felt the shock. "What a rotten thing to say."

He was silent for a while. "Being betrayed isn't just a woman's area. Wives and mothers have been known to abandon the marital home leaving devastation behind them. Women don't have a great deal of difficulty stamping on a man's heart."

Christy was taken aback by the degree of passion in his voice. "You're beginning to sound like a misogynist."

"Sometimes I think I am." He revealed a white twisted smile. "A reflection of my background perhaps. But to get back to you, Christy Parker, you could be a whole lot unhappier as an old maid."

"Don't use that term," she protested. "I'm a feminist, I don't like it. I'm sick of all the words men have thought up to label women."

"You don't think they deserve a lot of them?" he asked with strong sarcasm.

"Women don't need men," Christy said, sexual antagonism thick between them. "I suppose they might need them for an occasional bout of sex."

To her complete surprise given the tension between them, he burst out laughing. It was a very engaging sound. There were some things about him she managed to find wildly attractive. In desperation, not knowing what else to do in the presence of this complex man, Christy closed her eyes. Men of his type were new to her. He was too physically and verbally powerful. She was having such difficulty adjusting to everything that was happening. In a few short hours she'd gone from jilted woman and gatecrasher, to the new woman in Ashe McKinnon the cattle baron's life.

But then it was only play-acting.

Thank God.

"Wakey, wakey," a man's voice breathed seductively in her ear.

"Wh-a-at?" Christy started to say dazedly. "I surely didn't doze off?" She felt such confusion, disorientation, staring up into his fathomless dark eyes.

"You must have. You didn't notice when I kissed you."

"You didn't kiss me." She was absolutely certain she would have registered it. On the Richter scale. She understood already, miserable as she was, Ashe McKinnon was that sort of man.

"No, I didn't," he drawled. "I imagined I kissed you."

"Oh…" She was reduced to silence.

Seemingly like magic they were outside her apartment block, the surrounding well-kept gardens giving off the scent of gardenia and frangipani. Above her head the Southern Cross was a dazzling presence. It appeared to be right over the spot where she was standing. A billion stars gleamed. It was a heavenly night, velvety and fragrant. It made her feel very very sad. She even yawned. Ashe McKinnon and the chauffeur, however, had their two heads bent together.

What were they planning? Whatever Ashe said the chauffeur threw back his head and laughed. Men! They bonded in minutes. A moment more and the chauffeur got back behind the wheel, saluted briefly before he pulled away from the kerb, then did a U-turn back in the direction of the city.

''Well which is it?'' Ashe joined her, so tall he towered over her. ''The penthouse?'' He tilted his dark head back, staring up at the twenty floors of the high-rise building.

''Don't be stupid. I can't afford the penthouse,'' she said feeling a rush of something like panic, ''neither do I recall asking you in.''

''But my dear Miss Parker, it's totally expected under these circumstances. You need someone to look after you.''

''Not you, Mr. McKinnon. I'm in no doubt of that. Most decidedly not you.''

''That's okay.'' He answered casually as if he wanted no part of that agenda either. ''As it turns out I have plenty of women fighting over me.''

''Men who ooze money generally do.''

''Ouch, that was nasty.'' He made a mock attempt to defend himself. ''Come on, Miss Parker. For all you may have deserved it, you've had a bad day.'' He made a grab for her hand and momentarily defeated she let him take it again, curiously responding to the feel of those calluses against her smooth skin.

"Well if you're coming in for a while, come," she said, her voice carrying strain. " I want to get this damned dress off." It reminded her too bitterly of the wedding. Of wasted time. Failure.

He glanced down at her golden head for a moment then looked away. She'd created a sensation tonight. Ms. Bottecelli the gate-crasher. "Don't you think you're being rather forward?" he mocked.

She scarcely heard. "I can't stand it." There was nothing left to her but to mourn. Parting with ex-boyfriends was never easy even if they were hollow men. "I'll never give my heart again. I'll lock it away someplace inside me. I'll never give my trust."

"Oh stop feeling so sorry for yourself," he advised, not without pity. "You're young. You're beautiful. So you let yourself get involved with a villain, there are good guys out there. Next time," he added bluntly, "you might be a better judge. Callista spent more quality time choosing her wedding gown than her groom."

Whereas Josh the freeloader had instantly chosen a young woman with money to burn.

* * *

They never spoke in the lift. He looked marvellous, she thought somewhere between detachment and admiration. A prince among men. Josh couldn't hold a candle to him for looks or presence. Anything for that matter. If she was going to be fair. Not that Ashe McKinnon was the sort of man she should have fallen in love with. Men like that threw out such a challenge. One she preferred not to take on. Besides he was out of her league and he didn't believe in marriage either. A man like that would expect his bride to sign a watertight pre-nuptial contract.

Thinking about it, it only made common sense.

Christy reached out and dislodged the pink confetti on his shoulders thinking he'd probably look as wonderful in his working gear—akubra, bush shirt and jeans, riding boots on his feet—as a morning suit. Groovy. Really groovy. That's what her friend, Montana, would say. On the scale of one to ten Ashe McKinnon had to rate an eleven. She dwelt quietly on his physical attributes so as not to think about Josh. Josh would be labelled ''unfit'' beside this man.

''So what's the verdict?'' His eyes glinted.

''Sorry?'' They stepped out of the lift together, Christy indicating with a little flourish of her arm her apartment was the one to the far right.

''I'm surprised you haven't noticed my gold tooth.''

''You have a gold tooth?'' She stood stock-still and stared at him in horrified amazement.

''No I haven't, but if I had I'm sure you would have noticed it. Do you usually eyeball men so closely?''

''I know you look spectacular, but I was looking through you.''

''Here, give me that.'' She was fumbling, something she never did, but her fingers were nerveless, so he took the key off her, turning the dead lock and standing back while she preceded him into her one-bedroom but decidedly upmarket apartment. She would spend the rest of her life paying it off but it was an excellent investment.

Inside almost total darkness. He put out a hand and found the panel of light switches.

''How did you do that?'' She pushed back her hair.

''What?'' He gazed down at her with a puzzled expression.

"Find the lights so easily? I've never thought they were terribly well placed."

"I have X-ray vision. I've spent my life learning how to see in the dark."

"Ah the pleasures of being a cattle baron," she sighed. "Won't you sit down? I have to get out of this dress. Won't be a moment. Then we'll have coffee."

"Take your time," he said very dryly.

"What's so funny?" Christy turned back to ask.

"Oh life in the fast lane. Do you mind if I take off my cravat?"

"Go ahead." She met those eyes and had the extraordinary sensation something was cutting off her breath. "I'm not coming back in a negligee if that's what you're thinking. I intend to burn this dress."

"When I thought you should wear it forever," he said suavely. "I like your abode. Did you do the decorating yourself?"

"Right down to painting the walls. By myself. Now I think about it, Josh always had an excuse to avoid anything like physical hard work."

"You call painting a few walls hard work?" he called after her, his tone caustic.

Josh. Josh. Josh Deakin was *out* of her life.

''By the time I was finished I was burned out.''

Left alone Ashe wandered casually around the open-plan living-dining room. His study at home was bigger in area so he took small steps unless he powered into the sliding-glass doors that led out onto a small balcony. He went to the doors, opened them and stepped out to take a look at the view. Or city people called it a view. God, he could never live in the city, he thought for perhaps the millionth time. He could never be contained. But this was nice for what it was. A successful working girl's pad.

He wondered, with a surge of anger that could get him into trouble, whether Deakin had lived with her. Slept with her. Had his morning cup of coffee with her. He hoped not, picturing it but not wanting to.

The decor was entirely feminine yet a man would feel comfortable here. She had great taste, sensibility. Even unhappy she'd filled the place with flowers. He liked that. He liked the books she read. Lots of books. She would love the extensive library he had inherited with many important first editions and historical documents. His was one of the great pioneering families. He liked the prints on the walls. An oil painting of her. Very good. He understood the artist had been in love with her. It showed. He liked how everything was very clean, very neat. Orderly. She'd make a fine wife, he thought with a kind of dark amusement when in reality he was appalled she wanted Callista's brand-new husband. Yet when was the last time he'd found a woman so damned intriguing? Never was the answer. It left him feeling vaguely shell-shocked.

Finally he got his silk cravat undone and placed it on a side table. There was a glass bowl filled with beautifully perfumed yellow roses on it and a silver-framed photograph of her and he presumed her parents. She bore a strong resemblance to the woman, so youthful-looking she might have been an older sister but he knew she wasn't. The man was good-looking, too, rugged, with a look of character. For some reason he thought them landed people. Maybe they owned a farm of some sort. Living on the land was character building in his experience.

Ashe sank down into an armchair with apple green upholstery; spring colours dominated the room, awaiting the drama of her return. He was starting to wonder what the hell he thought he was doing? He wasn't the man to be swept away by a woman's very obvious charms. Correction: he hadn't been up to date. There was her beauty and the rest, the way she talked, the way she moved, but he realised he was getting too big a charge out of being with her.

He wanted her. The thought stunned him. He'd only just met her, under the worst possible circumstances, yet he wanted this woman. He supposed it was the way he lived his life. He was always making instant decisions. Big decisions. But he was never, couldn't afford to be, reckless. This was madness. So ill-advised. How could he possibly want a woman who was tearing herself to pieces over another man? A man moreover he already despised. Worse, married to his cousin. He knew better than anyone what happened to a man who let himself fall very deeply in love. It was like handing over one's soul. His mother had cheated on his father long before she finally left him. He couldn't get her treachery out of his head. More than twenty years later. His father was the finest man he had ever known. He had never grown another emotional layer of skin to enable him to remarry. His mother right up to the day he died had been enshrined in his father's memory. If it had been him...if it had been him...

"Oh dear, what's the matter?" Coming back into the room Christy gave him an alarmed glance. He looked positively daunting, the expression on his face dark and brooding.

"Nothing." He emptied his mind of all violence. "Do come further in and let me see you. Didn't change your mind? No negligee?" He spoke flippantly, trying to kill desire.

"You're a complete stranger." Just as coolly she answered his banter. She'd put on the first thing that came to hand, a pink-embroidered shirt over white cotton jeans. "Would you like coffee?"

"Coffee, the instant cure. Not the instant kind, I hope? You wouldn't by chance have any single malt whisky?"

Her face froze as memories floated up. "I let Josh have all his liquor back. I'm not much of a drinker. There is however a bottle of Tia Maria. It goes exactly with coffee."

"Tia Maria it is," he answered rather shortly, outraged anew by her feelings for Deakin. "It's not exactly what I planned but it will do. Strong, black coffee, no sugar. Do you need a hand?''

''There's not the space for you. How tall are you anyway?''

''If I remember correctly just over six-three. Are they your parents over there?'' He inclined his head towards the photograph.

''Yes.'' She came back into the living room, her beautiful face breaking into a smile. ''I miss them terribly.''

''Where are they?''

''I grew up on a sheep and lavender farm in Victoria. My parents are still there. They'll never leave. They adore country life and one another.''

''You're an only child?'' He stared at her with brooding eyes.

''Sad to say yes. My mother had a lot of trouble having me. My father couldn't have borne to lose her. That put paid to a bigger family. But I was never spoilt. I was never of the over-protective one-child syndrome. In fact I ran wild.''

''So you're a country girl?''

''Does that put me up a notch?'' She heard the approval in his voice.

''Indeed yes. When I marry—''

"To great applause," she cut in dryly.

"My wife will have to understand what living in the Outback means." His vibrant voice cracked right down the line.

"You look extremely sober when you say that," she commented.

"It's a top requirement." He didn't bare his soul to her. He didn't say his mother had been a beautiful social butterfly. A city girl, born and bred. In fact the last woman his father should have married. The last woman to mother a child. It was a miracle she had stayed so long. She had missed—expected to miss—his tenth birthday. There had been no celebration. His charming extravagant mother had run away. She was an adulteress, goddamn it. Love wouldn't stand between him and a successful marriage.

She brought him a hot steaming cup of excellent coffee along with a small crystal glass containing a dollop of liqueur.

"What are you having?"

"Aspirin." She couldn't disguise how she felt.

"Go back and get some coffee. Put a lot of milk in it," he ordered.

''You're the boss.'' She walked back into the kitchen and popped a small jug of milk into the microwave. ''I bet you're the boss even when you're asleep?''

''Of course I'm the boss. That's my job. So what next, Miss Parker?'' he asked, quietly surveying her.

''As in?'' Wearily she rubbed the faint cleft in her chin, taking a seat opposite him.

''Plans for the future. You realise you're going to have to cut Josh Deakin out of your life? End of story.''

''Obviously you haven't read my character correctly.'' She didn't know how it had happened but she desperately wanted him to approve of her.

''Not every ex-girlfriend turns up uninvited at a wedding.''

''Go on, rub it in.''

''I have to. I'm excessively biased in favour of my cousin.''

''She's a lucky girl.'' Christy gave a mournful sigh.

There was a little droop to her lovely mouth. It made him want to kiss it hard. A little punishment without hurting her. ''Anyway if you're a good girl and say your prayers, Mr. Right will come along.''

''Mr. Right?'' Her beautiful green eyes were distant. ''What makes men Mr. Right all of a sudden? I don't even want to talk about Mr. Right and marriage. I'm in denial.''

''I recognise that. I can even understand how you feel being burned. The fact is I'm wary of marriage myself.'' He said this with considerable self-mockery.

''Pray tell why is that? You don't look like you'd be wary of anything.''

''I've seen a lot of men lose their good judgment over a woman,'' he remarked cynically.

''Well you couldn't possibly say that only applies to men. Right now I'm feeling love is a four-letter word. And it definitely doesn't last. Well it did—it does—for my parents. But they're different.''

''You're thinking you don't stand a chance?'' He gave a quiet, ironic laugh. ''What about arranged marriages?'' he asked. ''Plenty of precedent for those. This head over heels bit doesn't always come off.''

''You can't be saying you'd seriously consider marrying a woman who doesn't love you?'' He took her breath away.

"And one I don't love either. I've no time for mad primitive urges, all that sweep a woman up and carry her off sort of stuff. One can learn to love, certainly. And, of course there must be trust and respect, mutual commitment and the same goals."

"Anything else?" She kept her eyes on him.

"Ideally she'll be good-looking, warm, compassionate, love kids, smart and able to take on a full partnership in the McKinnon operation. At least have input. I don't want any trophy wife."

"And one who would never be unfaithful?"

The brilliant black eyes turned glacial. "Why did you say that?" His handsome face tautened.

She took a little rapid breath. "I see it hit a nerve? You're certainly looking at me as though I'm not to be trusted."

"Women as beautiful as you mightn't make the safest wife," he retorted.

"Really?" Colour flared into her face. "You're a real woman hater, aren't you?"

"I'm just very much against divorce." He sounded deadly serious.

Christy half rose, anything but at ease with him. "More coffee?"

"No this is fine. You're not going to cry, are you? You've been very emotional all night."

"No I am not going to cry," she told him a little fiercely. "Dammit I don't understand men. You could have any woman you liked. That bridesmaid you were talking to? Did you happen to notice she's madly in love with you? And there were at least a dozen others sick with disappointment you had me hanging off your arm. Is it possible beneath that formidable exterior you're scared of women? Do you look like a panther when you're really a puppy?"

He surveyed her coolly. "I can't believe you said that. It's just that I want a lot, Christy. For one so recently jilted, you have a great deal to say."

The phone rang out, saving Christy an answer. They both jumped, so intcnsc was the atmosphere between them. Christy went to answer it. Who could be ringing her this time of night? Her mind sprang, instantly, anxiously, to her parents. Accidents happened on farms. Nerves tightening she spoke into the mouthpiece. "Christy here."

Silence at the other end then a man's voice so low she would have had to ask him to speak up only the voice was too familiar. "Christy, Christy, don't hang up."

Her heart contracted. Shock. Sick anger. Utter disbelief.

"Please...hear me out."

"You're kidding. You've got to be kidding!" The words burst from her before she could swallow them back. What sort of life form was he?

"Who is it?" Ashe McKinnon was on his feet. "Deakin?" His voice was hard.

She hung up immediately. "Don't be ludicrous. Wrong number. They were after a woman named Paderewski or Popadiamantris or someone."

He clicked his tongue disgustedly. "I can think of a few other things you might be but a good liar isn't one of them. We all know who Paderewski was and Papadiamantris to the best of my knowledge was a Greek writer. That was *Deakin*. Where in hell is he speaking from, the hotel? I'll go round."

That thoroughly panicked her. "I tell you, it was a wrong number."

The phone rang again but Ashe saved her the trouble of answering it. "McKinnon," he thundered. Straight from the Oval Office.

The very last thing Josh would have been counting on, Christy thought, secretly thrilled. Ashe McKinnon in her apartment. If McKinnon hadn't looked like he wanted to lynch someone she might have been able to laugh.

He hung up, obviously having frightened the caller off. "If Deakin were here right now he'd have to be hospitalised. It was him, wasn't it?" He drilled her with his brilliant stare.

"Don't jump to conclusions," Christy found herself imploring. Usually the people she dealt with were easy to handle. Not the cattle baron. No way. "It was the wrong number. I get lots of them."

He stared at her without a flicker of belief. "As an attempt at protecting your ex-boyfriend that was pitiful."

So it was, but the whole situation was highly explosive. And she was the cause of it. She should never have gatecrashed the wedding, no matter how badly Josh had treated her. "All right, then, I'm protecting Callista." She refused point-blank to be intimidated. "From you as much as him. Do you want to get back into town and punch him out? For all your talk of cool, common sense, you're a passionate man.'' She put out a hand and tentatively touched him. Much as a brave or alternatively stupid person would attempt to soothe a big cat. ''Please relax. Settle down.'' But settling down didn't appear to be on the agenda.

''They're supposed to be on their goddamn honeymoon and he's ringing you?'' he retorted in amazement. ''It's enough to make anyone reel.''

''It's been done before.'' She borrowed some of his own cynicism. ''Men ringing their mistresses and old girlfriends from the honeymoon suite. A crime of the heart. But it happens. The thing is you haven't got the right impression of me.''

''So educate me,'' he challenged, looking down that fine, straight nose at her.

''I can scarcely expect you to listen, you're so judgmental, but I don't, repeat, don't, fool around with married men. As far as I'm concerned, they're off-limits.''

''Fine words,'' he bit off edgily, his expression so infuriating, before she knew it, Christy's hand was in midair, carrying all the weight of her unhappiness behind it. He caught it, arresting her fiery reaction. ''Now there's a first,'' he said in very dangerous tones, as she stood there swaying. "No one has ever taken a swing at me before, much less a woman. I want to believe you, Christy Parker, but I have to say I'm absolutely rattled."

"Can't you appreciate it's the way I feel myself." She concentrated hard on rubbing her wrist. He hadn't hurt her applying just enough force to stop the blow but he had rendered her trembling. God knows what was at the heart of it. "This has been a dreadful day. A knock-out sort of day. I really should go to bed. Right now. This minute."

His brilliant eyes suddenly sparkled with black humour. "Maybe I should stick around in case you decide to call Deakin back?"

Pure melancholy was taking hold of her. "I can't believe how cruel you are," she murmured. "Not that I care. After tonight I'll never see you again."

He was aware how violently he wanted to change that. "You don't believe that any more than I do."

It was said in such a disturbing voice, with the irony she was becoming used to and something less identifiable. Whatever it was it sent shock waves through her. Feelings very hard to deal with on this day of days.

"I'll speak to you tomorrow." He sounded perfectly calm, even calculating.

"About what?" she asked bewilderedly, trying to find some clue in the unreadable depths of his eyes.

"Oh we'll go someplace," he tossed off carelessly. "I don't have to be back home until the end of the week." Not true but what the hell! He marvelled at how completely his focus had changed. "You need something to shake you out of your misery. You didn't love Deakin. No one could love anyone without a soul."

Soulless most of all. "I thought I loved him," Christy said, horrified when she felt tears well into her eyes. She couldn't cry in front of this man. She saw him as... Oh, God, what did she see him as? "You talk about a soul." She blinked back the tears furiously. "I can't even trust my own heart."

Again that white twisted smile. "You're not the first," he said with the faintest hint of grief. "Sometimes I think falling in love is a necessary evil. I know it's the reason I'm here. But we both might do better if we used our heads."

Christy stared away across the room. "I'm not that wise, I'm afraid. I'm not that cold-blooded either."

Desire was the most powerful allure of all. It had been drawing him inexorably to her all night. "No, your skin is like warm milk." He lifted her head, one hand beneath her chin, staring into her beautiful eyes, seeing himself reflected, instantly aroused by it. "In case you're going to lie awake all night thinking how awful life is and how much you still love Deakin, why don't I give you something else to dwell on?"

With his other arm he folded her strongly to him, then he kissed her mouth. Almost gently at first, tasting her lips, savouring them, then more fully, deeply opening her lips like petals to find the sweet nectar.

It was the faultless execution of a kiss by a master. A kiss that would keep her awake for hours. Her heart fluttered wildly, a pretty song-bird crammed into a cage. There were flick-ering lights behind her eyes indicating a high degree of arousal. She knew on one level he was punishing her, but he was effortlessly en-gineering a response.

She felt it, all along her body. Her face, her throat, her breasts, her thighs. Electric tingles raced lightning-quick, along her limbs, stirring up a heat that moved to the pit of her stomach and the glowing crux of her body. It was a kiss the likes of which she had never known.

When he finally withdrew his mouth she could hear the rasp of his breath. She feared he could hear her own involuntary little moans. She was trembling with an effort to absorb all these new sensations. What had he been attempting here? Whatever it was he had proved his point. Or was proving a point all that it was? She couldn't find words to ask. He had stolen all her breath.

He took her hands, stood with her while they both quietened. ''I think that had results.'' There was a decided edge of self-mockery in his voice. ''I don't imagine it's restored your faith in life, but at least it shook you up a little.''

Like an earth tremor. She stared up at him with brooding eyes. ''I never asked for that.''

He gave her that ironic white smile she was fast coming to look for. ''Who knows, it might have been destined.''

She looked away. "At least I have to thank you for stopping me from making an utter fool of myself." A solitary tear slid down her cheekbone.

Ashe gathered it with his finger and put it into his mouth. "There, gone," he said a little harshly. "No more tears for Deakin."

"I have to swear to it?" she asked quietly.

This time the smile seemed to cost him an effort. "You do. Repeat after me. I, Christy Parker—"

She let him have what he wanted. He had wanted her mouth. "I Christy Parker—"

"Will never allow Joshua Deak—"

"Will never allow Joshua Deakin—"

"Into my heart again." He blurred the anger. "Moreover I will never do anything to threaten or destroy his marriage."

She winced. The tip of her tongue moistened her tingling lips.

"Say it." His expression was still very serious and strangely dark.

She obeyed, quite under his spell. "I will never do anything to threaten or destroy his marriage. There, does that satisfy you? Because I can't take a minute more." Not at this level of intensity. The male scent of him was all over her; warm, clean, intoxicating.

"Vows you'll disobey at your peril." The dark shadows gradually left his face. "That's over, I'll let you go to bed, Christy. You're out on your feet." He turned to find his cravat, picking it up and shoving it in his pocket.

"How are you getting back?" she roused herself to ask. "Let me call a cab."

"Don't bother." He looked down at the hand she had placed spontaneously on his arm. "I can walk."

"It's too far," she shook her head. "Miles." She knew he was staying with Mrs. Mercedes McKinnon.

"You don't seem to remember I'm from the Outback," he scoffed. "Your idea of miles is a hop, step and a jump. Besides I have a few blunt corners in my head to knock off. A walk will do me good." He turned at the door. Tall, elegant, vital, scornful. A man like that could rock a woman to her very core.

"I'll ring you around ten tomorrow. We'll go out for the day. Take a drive, the ocean, the mountains, have lunch somewhere. Okay?"

Who could argue with the man? Compliance was a natural response.

CHAPTER THREE

IN THE morning, it took Christy some time before she could actually look herself directly in the eyes. This time yesterday she didn't even know Ashe McKinnon. This time yesterday she'd considered herself a woman in a sorry plight, betrayed by the man she thought loved her, ready to cause him some fright by gate-crashing his wedding. What was she now? Apparently about as fickle as they come. The very thought seared her with shame and embarrassment. At the same time as she thought she was agonizing over Josh's betrayal another man was making an enormous impression on her. Was that normal? Or would any woman succumb to such a dynamic man?

She was still feverishly working on that when the phone rang.

''So how did the wedding go?'' her friend Montana greeted her with bated breath. ''Did you give him a damned good fright? On the other hand, did you get thrown out? I see nothing in the papers except a lot of gush over the bride and her filthy-rich folks.''

''You really want to know?'' Christy asked. She had confided in Montana about an hour before she had left for the wedding, Montana, being Montana, had egged her on.

''Why do you think I'm ringing? I'm dying to know.'' A crunching sound. ''That was an apple,'' Montana explained.

Christy told her friend in detail, even down to the table decorations. She didn't excuse Josh for his unforgivable behaviour. She told Montana all about the reception. How Ashe McKinnon had saved her from...

''Aaah!'' Montana interrupted theatrically, obviously visualising the whole scenario. ''Ashe McKinnon! I've always wanted to meet a man called Ashe McKinnon and a cattle baron! Lucky, lucky you. If I didn't love you I'd hate you for being so beautiful and never putting on weight. That's a sore point with me.''

''Do you want to hear?' Christy asked patiently. Montana had a delicious curvy figure but she couldn't live without her bathroom scales. And her apple diets.

''Throw it at me,'' Montana invited.

"Then I'm not so lucky. He was doing it all for his cousin. He's extremely fond of her."

"Oh don't give me that!" Montana retaliated. "You're the sort of woman to drive men mad. Personally I think it's just an over-rated thing, long blond hair."

"You may well be right. Josh wasn't going to commit to it. Or me," Christy pointed out, with a sick twist of the heart. "He quickly stepped away from me for a girl with more money."

"Okay so Josh Deakin is a scumbag," Montana reasoned. "I had to pretend I didn't mind him."

"You did a remarkably good job." Christy was only half joking.

"But, darling, you thought you were in love with him," Montana cried as though that explained everything. Perhaps it did. "What was the point of saying anything? I had to leave well alone. We all did. Thank God you've had a lucky break. You can start again. Stitch up an affair with this McKinnon guy."

"Sorry, too dangerous." Though Montana couldn't see her, Christy shook her head vigorously.

"I bet he's real groovy?"

"You should see him," Christy said very dryly.

"And he's a true-blue, red-blooded bloke?" Montana joked.

"I think anything else is pretty rare in the Outback."

"I want to see him," Montana crowed. "Do you think I might be tempted?"

"Absolutely. I'd be tempted myself if I hadn't had such a bad experience."

"And just how many do you think I've had dished out to me?" Montana asked. "Five? Six?" Montana gave her gutsy, infectious laugh. "It's really sad you had to find out the hard way about Josh, honey, but something wonderful is in store for you. Remember what they used to say about you at Uni? You'd end up Someone."

"Spoken by the woman who voted for me."

"So what's the cattleman like in bed?" Montana screeched with laughter.

"I'm quite sure he's absolutely fabulous," Christy replied.

"Oh God, you must have fallen in love with him?"

"It's hard to fall in love with someone when you're still trying to recover from a broken heart,'' Christy offered very soberly. Although Josh had failed dismally to measure up, it didn't lessen the wounded pride.

''Don't let it warp you, kiddo,'' Montana advised gently. ''So, are you going to see the cattle baron again?''

''We're going out for the day actually,'' Christy confided, thinking the way she was acting was really odd. Maybe it was natural after emotional shock. ''I'm waiting on his call.''

''How about that!'' Montana let out another excited shriek. ''So, didn't I tell you, you can always take the next cab on the rank. I'll get off in case he rings. Give me a buzz tonight, eh, kiddo?''

''Will do.'' Christy blew a kiss down the phone.

When Ashe McKinnon's call came she had to rush out of the shower to answer it, wrapping herself in a towelling robe trying to compose herself.

''How are you today?'' he asked, solicitous but with a bite.

She had a vivid mental image of him. ''I'm fine.'' She was doubly aware, too, of his very attractive voice. Voices were very important to her. His exactly fitted his image. Fascinating, deep, dark, vibrant, kind of edgy.

"So have you decided where you'd like to go?"

"Does this come under the category of keeping an eye on me?" Christy challenged.

"It might well do, Christy, but also I like having your company. Would you consider the beach? I don't see much of the blue Pacific where I come from. More like endless miles of desert and towering blood-red sand hills."

"Uluru is one of my favourite places on earth," the much-travelled Christy told him with a rush of enthusiasm. She had nominated the most famous monolith of the Red Centre. "But the beach is great. Josh and I used to—" She broke off too late, disgusted with herself for the slip.

"Do you really think I want to hear?" Antagonism threaded his voice.

"I was talking without thinking. I need time to get rid of the old baggage. Time to lose the cruel cuts and bruises."

"Josh, my dear Christy, has met and married someone else," he pointed out. "As I've said before, you'd better dash all thoughts of him from your mind. The fact is you made vows remember?''

''Vows you're obviously going to hold me to,'' she said with a little latent hostility.

''I expect you to hold to them yourself. We can talk everything through later in the day if you like. My cousin, Nicole, has a beach house at Noosa—she and her husband, Brendan. You may remember them from last night. I did introduce you.''

Christy considered all the people she had met. Usually she remembered everybody. ''I don't think so! I wasn't at my sharpest last night.''

''Well they remember you.'' His tone was as dry as hers, more sarcastic. ''Nicole is under the impression you've stolen my heart.''

''Instead of causing you concern!'' she retorted. ''I do remember now. Nicole and Brendan, of course. Brendan is an architect? We only spoke for a moment but I liked them. It struck me Nicole has very sad eyes.''

There was silence for a moment, then his quiet voice. ''That's very perceptive, Christy. Nic lost her baby earlier in the year. She was ill herself for a time. Complications for mother and child. The little girl survived a day or two. They were devastated.''

Sympathy welled up in her. ''Oh, they would be. I'm so very sorry. It puts my heartbreak into perspective.''

''Except your heart isn't broken.'' The gentle, almost tender tone toughened. ''Your pride has been dashed, that's all. You'll realise that more and more as the weeks go on. Anyway,'' he continued bracingly, ''Nic asked us up for lunch if we care to go. If you're shy or you prefer not to, we can go our own way.''

''I'm not a shy person,'' she assured him.

He thought of the way she had returned his kiss. The touch and taste of her mouth. ''I know that, Christy. Being shy would seem implausible for such a beautiful woman—''

''Let alone a valued member of a top P.R. firm.''

''Ah, yes. Whitelaw Promotions, isn't it?'' he asked suavely.

''You have a good memory.''

''It came to me in a flash. And then there were the photographers although we tried to dodge them. One called out to you, 'Christy, look this way!'''

"We turn up at the same functions," she explained lightly. "So, it's lunch with Nichole and Brendan?"

"I think you'll enjoy it. Nic is a brave girl. They have two other children. Great little kids, Kate's six. I'm her godfather. Kit—Christopher—is four."

"We have something in common already, a name." A smile sounded in Christy's voice.

"A beautiful name." He said it in such a way it gave her a little shiver. "You'll still want to bring your bikini. I have every intention of hitting the surf."

The Boyds' contemporary beach house, a house of dynamic forms, commanded a rocky hilltop overlooking the glorious ocean.

"What a magnificent site," Christy remarked, staring up at it from the road. They had been driving for well over an hour and now they were due to arrive.

"As you can see, the house takes full advantage of the view," Ashe acknowledged with a smile. "Brendan designed it. They always wanted a house at the beach. Especially when the kids came along. The Pad they call it."

''Some pad!'' She reflected for a moment who could afford it. And it was the second house.

He laughed. ''Actually though the front facade is quite striking I prefer the house as seen from the beach. It's like a giant sculpture. An extension of the cliff face.''

''It's certainly very large.'' And it spelled money. No one could build a house like that without a family fortune.

''I suppose it is,'' he agreed casually, used to a huge historic homestead from childhood. ''The west wing is for family or guests when they come visiting. Nic's father is a career diplomat. He has a posting overseas. The U.S. of A. They love it. Nic doesn't see much of her parents these days. Her mother is the McKinnon. My late father's sister, Caroline. He had three. One visits me every so often, Zoe. She's a real character, an academic never married, but with plenty of interests. The other was killed in a fall from her horse when she was only sixteen. The fall didn't kill her. The horse took fright and kicked her in the head.''

''How terrible.'' So not such a fortunate life. Christy stared away, knowing how tragic for the family that must have been.

He nodded, his handsome face taking on its somewhat severe expression. "My grandparents never got over it. At least they didn't live to face the loss of their two sons. My father and Callista's. They were killed in a light plane crash, mechanical failure. It simply fell out of the air."

The tender-hearted Christy felt like reaching for his hand but didn't dare. "So life has been cruel?"

"Very much so, in some ways. At one time I thought it was going to be a way of life." Grief flickered like a shadow.

"And your mother? Does she live on the station?" Christy turned her head to look at him. Perfectly straight nose, chiselled mouth, strong chin and jawline. He was a profoundly handsome man.

"My mother left when I was ten years old," he said, to her surprise. She hadn't read about that. "Almost to the day."

It was said without expression. Yet Christy looked down at her hands. Some intonation in his voice warned her not to ask the reason.

"She was desperate to start a new life," he explained after a fraught pause. She was going to hear it sooner or later anyway. "My mother was bored to distraction with the isolation. Staring out at the horizon. She's a city girl born and bred, she needs lots of lights and entertainment.''

Bitterness and indifference were equally balanced. ''Your parents divorced?'' Christy asked quietly.

''Of course, Christy.'' He threw her a brilliant satirical glance. ''My mother remarried. With a speed that startled us all. Later we found out she was pregnant.''

''Oh!'' Well that explained the flight and the haste. ''So you have a half brother or sister.''

''Apparently,'' he said.

God knows what was behind that shut expression. ''You don't know them?'' Christy, a much-loved only child, couldn't believe it.

''Once or twice I thought I'd like to know them,'' he admitted. ''It's a brother by the way. Duane Moss Huntington III.''

So his mother hadn't run off with an ordinary man.

''But you saw your mother after?'' she asked, agonizing for all of them. His mother would have applied for joint custody. It occurred to her he must have been a most beautiful ten-year-old, curly dark hair and those wonderful eyes. No mother could turn her back on such a child. Any child of her flesh.

"For a while," he shrugged, the mask firmly in place. "My visits weren't successful. I detested her husband, and sad to say, I despised her. I was very difficult. At war with everyone. My main desire was to get away from them and back to my father."

"It's only natural it very much affected you."

The shapely mouth compressed. "For quite a while I must have been out of control. I don't really remember. But eventually it was something I had to accept. And I did. It was my father who couldn't accept his beautiful wife had left him. He loved her. He'd been so proud of her. She had everything a woman could want, but she threw it back in his face."

"Where does she live now?" Christy asked quietly, an answering ache starting up in her.

"California and New York mainly, though they spend time in Europe. Her husband is an exceptionally rich man. Even richer than my dad, though she swore it was love. Love, my God!"

"We can't protect ourselves against it," she offered sadly, her mind crammed all of a sudden with images of her faithless Josh. "Love takes hold of us regardless of wisdom, or even will. Sometimes it never lets go."

"It never let go for my father though I was wild enough in those days not to have made a good stepson. I wanted my own mother back as she was, not a stranger. But what she did was unforgivable in my book. So terribly, terribly cruel." How well he remembered the loneliness his father had endured, the heartbreak. Men didn't ease their feelings with tears.

"You think she should have stayed?"

That roused him. "Yes I do. I know duty is an old-fashioned word but she should have tried to live up to her vows."

"So vows are very important to you?"

"Enormously important." He shot her a sardonic glance. "Please, Christy, spare me the psychoanalysis. People shouldn't get married if they're not prepared to bring everything they've got to that commitment."

"Yet it still goes wrong," she lamented. "That is to say people change. Grow in different directions. Men are the worst offenders in my book. A lot of them go for a stream of women. They have to prove endlessly they're virile. I had absolutely no idea Josh was seeing your cousin until the evening I happened to pass by the law courts and saw them together, kissing.''

''What did you do, throw a rock?'' He glanced at her swiftly, black eyes sardonic.

''Would it have helped? No, I went on my way. I confronted him the next day.''

''And what did he say?''

He actually slowed the Mercedes, his aunt's, who liked the notion of a namesake car, to ponder her answer, but he was the very last person outside Callista Christy thought she could tell. ''He explained he didn't love me anymore.'' She saw no option but to tell the saving white lie.

''Why do I find it hard to accept that?'' he groaned.

''That's the way it was. I expect he rang last night to apologise for not acknowledging me at the reception.''

''You know that's exactly what he said.'' The mockery was very much on the grim side.

''Meaning?'' She stared across at him.

''You don't really think I was going to let that phone call go. I don't like people who play dirty. People who try to put things over my family. Deakin needed to be warned off.''

"You surely didn't go to the hotel?'' Christy felt the quake in her body.

"Listen I would have got into bed with them if it would have helped,'' he exploded. "I made a call from the lobby. Your Josh hurried down.''

"He isn't my Josh.'' Christy made the heated response.

"He surely isn't,'' he retorted just as smartly, "but that doesn't make me feel a helluva lot better.''

"So what did you say to him?'' Christy shuddered, conjuring up the scene.

"Among other things, Miss Parker, I told him he wouldn't want to make an enemy out of me.''

"Okay, I don't want to make an enemy out of you,'' she said. "I'm for a quiet life.''

"I suggest you'll only have a quiet life when you're very very old. All Deakin could think of was protecting himself. At your expense, anyone's expense, and that goes for Callista. I don't give this marriage six months.''

No part of Christy was pleased, something she would later come to appreciate was telling. Now she said, "Did anyone ever tell you you're a very cynical man? Callista might just love him enough to turn him around. She seems like a very loving person, sweet and gentle…"

"Close up Callista can also be tough," he said in an ironic voice. "She's not a McKinnon for nothing."

"What do any of us know about anyone." Christy shrugged, sounding upset.

He reached over to touch her hand. "Please don't, Christy. I want you to be happy."

The charm—all the more powerful because it wasn't turned on—made her heart flip over in her breast. "You can be nice when you want to," she said as though delivering a difficult verdict.

"There are lots of things about you I like," he answered. "That little cleft in your chin, that long beautiful hair and the clear light green of your eyes. I like their slant. The rest of you isn't bad either."

"So what don't you like? Maybe you'd better not answer, I don't want to jeopardize the day."

''I don't like the way you chose a guy like Josh Deakin to fall in love with. I would have thought you had better taste. Not only taste. I thought you were a woman more in control.''

''So I've burnt my fingers,'' Christy said in a slightly combative tone. ''Next time I start a relationship with a man, a whole lot of planning is going to go into it.''

''What about a man you don't love? And who doesn't love you. Then no one will get hurt.'' He glanced at her, a devastating quirk to his mouth.

''Sorry, I'd have to be attracted to him.''

''Naturally,'' he nodded, ''otherwise you'd need your head examined. Why don't you sit down one day and itemise your requirements?''

If she did the list wouldn't contain words that fit him. Like difficult, dangerous, gut-wrenchingly exciting, complex, a man who kept a tight rein on his volatile emotions.

''Shame on you, Christy,'' he drawled, as if reading her mind. He turned his head and gave her a smile.

Ashe McKinnon. Smiles like that even a jilted woman could get hooked on.

* * *

The children were the first to greet them, flying out the front door, running so fast Christy was concerned there would be a fall and very possibly tears. It would be no surprise.

''Uncle Ashe, Uncle Ashe!'' they cried in unison, their faces reflecting so much happiness it gave Christy yet another insight into this complex man. For one thing it showed he loved kids and they dearly loved him. The little girl, the elder, had no trouble negotiating the driveway lined by Royal Cuban palms with a triangular section of lush green lawn, but the small boy, just as Christy feared, took a tumble, mercifully on the soft turf.

Ashe, who had gathered Kate's flying figure into his arms, looked away in time to see Christy rush to Kit who lay face down, spread-eagled, apparently kissing the grass.

''Poppet, that was quite a tumble.'' Christy bent over the child who turned an adorable little face to her, inky-black curls in contrast to sapphire-luminous blue eyes.

''Oh I don't mind flying but I've got all this grass down my throat.'' The little boy sat up and gave a choke while Christy patted him on the back.

"What about a glass of water?" she suggested, already half rising.

"No that's okay," Kit vigorously spat grass clippings out of his mouth. "I'm all right." In fact he looked all buoyed up by their arrival. "Are you Christine?"

"Christy to my friends." She gave him her hand, not really expecting him to shake it, perhaps take it, but he pumped away happily.

"You've got a name like mine. Congratulations."

"I'm sure it means we're going to be friends."

"Oh yes, you're the prettiest lady I've ever seen, 'cept Mummy. You can call me Kit. Mummy calls me that."

"It's a great nickname!" Christy stood up, bringing the little boy with her. Kit's beaming smile faded.

"Oh look what I've done! I've made a mark on your skirt. It must have been when I was spitting."

Christy looked down, while the sapphire eyes focused anxiously on her. "That's fine. It will rub off. In fact it's almost disappeared." She shook a tiny mound of damp green grass clipping off her jade cotton skirt, which she wore with a matching halter top.

"Oh good," said Kit, grinning broadly, taking possession of her hand. "I told Daddy not to cut the grass but he said he wanted it to be nice. He put the sprinkler on, too. That's why the grass is wet. I slipped."

"Anyone could have slipped," Christy assured the little boy, making him glow.

"Yes!" he agreed happily. "Though Katey never falls over. You've come with Uncle Ashe. Do you love him?" he shot her a surprisingly searching look.

What to say? Up until yesterday I fancied myself in love with the man who married one of your cousins? "You know what a secret is, don't you, Kit?" Christy said finally, speaking in a low confidential voice.

"What big people won't tell you about?"

"Until it's time," Christy nodded. "But I will tell you I like him very much." She didn't mean that at all. Ashe McKinnon wasn't the sort of man one simply liked.

"That's good," Kit said approvingly. "Uncle Ashe is ours. Mummy said he takes care of us all. I wish we were at home, I could show you my goldfish." He held her hand so

naturally he might have been holding her hand
for all of his short life. ''Come and meet Kate.
That's her flapping her hands. I don't like it
when she beats me to Uncle Ashe. She always
gets ahead because she's so big.''

''Being a boy means you'll be taller than
her pretty soon,'' Christy pointed out.

''I'll never be as tall as Uncle Ashe,'' Kit
lamented, thrusting out his chest. ''He's loads
taller than Daddy. Of all our relations I love
him the best.''

And there had to be lots of reasons, Christy
thought, walking with Kit toward the other
two.

''So how's my little pal?'' Ashe called, suddenly tumble-turning a squealing Kate to the
ground. Kit ran to him and got hoisted onto
Ashe's shoulder.

''Why haven't you brought Christy before?'' He cupped Ashe's face and bent his
dark head to talk into his uncle's ear. ''Christy
wouldn't tell me if she loved you or not. It's
a secret.''

''That's all right, Kit. She hasn't told me
either. Come on, Katey, we haven't forgotten
you. Get yourself around here.'' He reached

back and caught her. "Christy this is my little god-daughter—"

"Favourite god-daughter," Katey corrected sweetly, very much like her brother in features, build and colouring.

"Favourite god-daughter—I was about to say that—Katherine McKinnon Boyd."

"That was Mummy's name," Katey told Christy, coming to take her hand. "It makes me special."

"I can see that. My name is Christine Prudence Parker."

"What?" Ashe turned to stare at her.

"Why not?" She returned his glance. "If you really liked me you wouldn't mind."

"Only you're fooling, aren't you?" Katey smiled up at her. "It's not really Prudence?"

"Actually it is." Christy grimaced a little. "I had a great-aunt Prudence. She was going to leave me her magnificent four-poster bed, with all the trimmings, one day, but she never did."

"Who got it?' Katey looked at her aghast.

"I bet there are about forty cats on it right now," Christy said. "Aunt Pru was a great cat fancier. She left her home and all her money to her companion on the understanding she would look after her cats.''

Ashe guffawed and the children bent double.

''What's going on?'' a woman's voice called, hearing all the laughter.

''Oh, Mummy. Come and meet Christy,'' Katey begged. ''She's lovely!''

''Hi, Christy.'' Nicole, dark-haired, blue-eyed, was all smiles. ''Hi, Ashe. I'm so glad you came. Brendan is in the house burning something on the stove. Honestly it's enough to make you cry, but he fancies himself as a chef.''

''If the worse comes to the worst, we can always go to a restaurant.'' Ashe laughed, bending to kiss his cousin's cheek.

''Only joking,'' Nicole said. ''How lovely you look, Christy. Bren and I weren't sure we dreamed you last night.''

''You're being very kind to me.'' Christy met the smiling gaze, wishing she didn't have to deceive this friendly young woman about the exact nature of her relationship with Ashe. ''I can see where the children get their beautiful sapphire eyes.''

"The eyes are mine," Nicole said fondly. "The rest of them is all Bren. Please, come inside." She curled her arm through Christy's. "I thought Ashe told me everything but he didn't tell me about you."

"It's a secret, that's why." Kit's voice rose. "Christy is not ready to say."

"Ho-ho-ho-ho," was Nicole's response. "We'll get it out of her."

In fact they never did, increasing the high level of interest. But then Ashe was very very deep.

It turned out to be a surprisingly lovely day full of peace, harmony, sunshine and surf, with delightful well-mannered children impossible not to like. A great lunch was prepared by Brendan, with everyone serving themselves from a table in the kitchen and carrying their plates out onto the patio with its glorious views of the beach, the ocean and the hinterland. There was a magnificent red emperor, caught only that morning, baked whole with a saffron sauce, John Dory in beer batter, which the children loved, served with lashings of delicious homemade chips, grilled chicken with an Oriental flavour in case Christy was one of those rare Australians who didn't like sea-food—of course she did—accompanied by a garden fresh salad with a difference—Parmesan-crisped fingers of focaccia, again a favourite of the children.

"It's marvellous to see them enjoying salad," Christy remarked to Nicole, watching the two little people eating it enthusiastically. "I have friends with small children who agonize over not being able to get the kids to eat vegetables let alone salad."

"We started them very early," Brendan, a very attractive thirty-two-old, explained. "This was the food we all ate and miracle of miracles they accepted it."

"What a blessing!" Christy smiled. "They're beautiful children. A great credit to you both."

"We lost one." Nicole's light charming voice suddenly broke, betraying the sad fact the loss was eating away at her.

Christy grasped her hand and held tight. "I know. Ashe told me. I'm so sorry. Truly so sorry. I can only guess at your heartbreak."

Nicole tried very hard to regain control. "But hey, I wasn't going to mention that, was

I?'' She glanced at her husband who smiled at her with love and understanding.

''You're allowed to mention it, Nic,'' Ashe told her quietly. ''We all love you here.''

''That includes me,'' Christy added affectionately. It could easily become true. Nicole drew her as a person.

Later they all went down to the beach where Ashe and Christy had their work cut out trying to get out of the shallows where the children, being children, wanted their full attention. Finally, Brendan came to their rescue, extending both hands.

''Hey, you two, Ashe and Christy have been really good to you and now it's their turn to have a swim. Let's make a space station and give them a surprise.''

The children trotted off with their father while Ashe shot Christy a challenging look. ''So do I need to give you a head start? I don't know if the costume can take it.''

''Of course it can take it! Versace lycra. Like it?'' Soothed by the lovely day, Christy laughingly struck a model's pose. She'd been hanging out at the beach since she'd been a child. She kept herself in very good shape. Why shouldn't she be at ease in a brief

Tigerlily bikini even with those brilliant dark eyes on her?

"The word is love. I love it," he mocked.

"Thank you."

For the next half hour they revelled in the blue crystal water. Christy, a strong swimmer, moved out with him to the front line of the body surfers shooting the big foaming waves right in to the shore. The two of them stayed close together, a seemingly spontaneous thing. It was marvellous. Christy would have liked to spend the rest of the afternoon with the two of them swimming together. Out to the horizon, she thought blissfully. She was used to long swims. She had always stayed in much longer than Josh—in fact Josh didn't swim as well as she did. She couldn't say that of Ashe McKinnon, causing her to wonder how and where he got in his swimming in his desert home. Back on the warm white sand, she asked.

"Good grief, we have lagoons." He looked at her in amazement, picking up her towel and handing it to her. "Chains of beautiful, coolabah-lined billabongs crisscross the station. In the bad times many are reduced to a mere trickle but others are deep permanent waterholes and bracingly cold. I'd rather swim there than anywhere else outside the ocean. We have a swimming pool, too, for the convenience of our guests.''

''The unadventurous ones?'' She lightly towelled herself off. The sun would do the rest.

''It's true some people are overawed by the wilderness and the sheer size of the place. Two million acres. We have a thriving live cattle export market with Malaysia and Egypt going at the moment with 100 million riding on it. A lot of people connected to the industry come and go. We also breed the Australian workhorse, a descendant of the Waler. They're splendid animals with good temperaments, so they're very much in demand for workhorses—the best—and polo ponies. All in all, we do a lot of entertaining in connection with the operation.''

''So you really need a wife, a hostess?'' She turned an enquiring face to him, unnerved by something in his expression.

''Would you care to discuss it with me?''

''What would be the point?'' she answered flippantly, but she shook inside. ''I told you. I'm off marriage as a topic of discussion. For a long time.''

''What a challenge!'' The self-assurance in his black eyes brushed that claim aside. ''Do you know how good you look?'' He reached out and touched the back of her neck. Her warm, thick, golden hair, honey-coloured when wet, was arranged in a long, thick plait so her nape was bare, creamy to his touch.

For Christy, the cobalt-blue sky tilted.

His hand on her skin, the strong pads of his fingers.

She experienced a blind rush of sexuality.

He knew how to touch a woman. Years of practice? Just a stroke, yet her insides clenched. Such an erotic sensation. He was so much taller than she. So much darker of skin. The skin of her salt-glossed body was palest gold against his dark tan. It appeared to be all over. No paler line of skin anywhere. He had a splendid physique. So arrogantly male. All of a sudden Christy had an overpowering impulse to just fall to the sand and lie there in front of him. Could it be she was emotionally unstable? Worse, was she transparent?

Even as her thoughts confused and disturbed her, he pulled her to him and kissed her mouth. Kissed her. *Kissed her.* Kisses didn't get any better. Or so memorable.

"Do you mind?" he murmured as he finally lifted his dark head.

"You could explain what that was all about." While she was almost blind to her surroundings, he glanced casually over her head.

"Nic and the kids are coming back from their walk. They'll expect to see me kissing you. They think you're my girl."

"We could correct that in a minute," she said sharply. "We could tell them the truth."

"The one thing we can't do." He began to slowly unplait her hair, and shook it loose. "Not now. Let's keep this day as happy as we can."

She nodded after a minute and stared at the three figures in the distance. "Nicole is trying so hard to be brave but she's hurting badly inside."

He shrugged a powerful shoulder. "She's not as well as I thought." His expression deepened into concern.

"Maybe there's such a thing as trying too hard to carry on," Christy said quietly. "Forgive me if I'm being presumptuous but I think Nic needs more time to grieve. Brendan, too. I can see how much they love each other. He's doing everything he can to help."

"He's a good man." Ashe gave his hard-muscled body a token rubover with his towel. "Nic couldn't have married anyone better. What they both need is a complete break. I'll speak to them. The kids would adore to come outback."

That was a big surprise. "Could you manage them? I had the idea you were an extremely busy and committed man."

"That's where *you* come in," he said.

"Me?" She experienced a sharp fierce moment of shock and glanced up at him quickly; stunned to see he was serious.

"You probably don't remember but you let slip in the car you were owed a month off?"

She floundered. "I certainly didn't intend spending it with you in your desert stronghold. I'm far from ready for such an experience."

"It would certainly keep you away from your ex-lover," he said, the note of humour off key.

"I thought they were supposed to be on their honeymoon?" Christy shot back.

"Three weeks isn't long. I don't trust that guy."

"As it turns out, neither do I," she said, still retaining the pain of hurt and humiliation.

"My pride has been badly dented. Remember I was jilted."

"Jilted?" He was roused to throw up his high-mettled head. "When he's so damn desperate to get you for his mistress?"

Only the truth. "I'm glad the children aren't with us," she told him severely.

"You will forgive me, I hope?" His sardonic gaze rested on her upturned face, the cream skin deepened a little by the golden rays of the sun. "By the way, how come you didn't arrive at an engagement? Or did you and you've given back the ring?"

"Oh God, let's have a nice afternoon?" she groaned, trying to hold back a cloud of windblown hair.

"*I'm* having a great time." He informed her. "You're quite athletic, aren't you?"

"I won lots of prizes at school," she answered. It was true.

"With a tendency to boast."

Christy had to laugh. "I'm not out to impress you. I'm just telling it the way it was. Dressage was an interest for a while."

"Really?" One black brow shot up. "Now that does have a certain cachet, Christy."

''Farm girl,'' she responded. Horses were a way of life.

''Size of the farm?''

''Oh, close to a thousand acres. A speck compared to your little spread.''

''I see gold and green.'' He smiled. ''Rolling hills. Fields of wheat. Woolly sheep.''

''Beautiful lucent mists in the morning. Sounds like you've been there.''

''I've been just about everywhere in the pastoral world,'' he told her, joining her on the sand. ''Perhaps. Perhaps...'' He looked off pensively towards the sparkling ocean. The surface was spread with glittering diamonds. Seagulls swooped in search of food; foaming white water washed the sand.

''What?'' she prompted. Of course she was meant to be intrigued. She knew that but still she was caught hook, line and sinker.

''I've just had a profound thought. Is it possible you'd consider helping me if I offer to take the kids? I promise I'll do everything to make your stay on Augusta exciting and enjoyable.''

Under the cover of her wide-brimmed straw hat, Christy's face flushed. Augusta Downs, his station. ''You can't be serious?''

"I'm accustomed to speaking seriously," he informed her, giving her what she was coming to think of as his "lordly" look.

"Then why have you sprung this on me now?" she demanded, turning sideways to stare at him.

"Surely because I only just thought of it. Okay—" he shrugged "—I had considered getting *you* to the station but that was before I came to fully appreciate how down Nic really is."

Christy's expression matched her feverish green eyes. "Don't you think this is just a teeny-weeny bit impetuous?" she suggested. "First and foremost, Nic being a most loving and conscientious mother mightn't consent to such a thing. After all they barely know me. *You* don't know me either for that matter, although you seem to be arranging my life."

His eyes moved along her beautiful pale gold legs. Like a ballet dancer's, slender but strong. "I'm in my element arranging things," he said dryly.

"You're a terrible person."

His dark eyes gentled. "You're not joking! Don't you want to do a good deed?"

She sighed deeply. ''I don't understand you, Ashe McKinnon. Yesterday you were angered by the very sight of me.''

''Did I really give you that impression?'' This creature of grace and beauty? Elegant lines and beguiling curves.

''Yes, you did,'' she said, cramming the flower-decorated straw hat further down on her head.

His mouth twisted ironically. ''I didn't want to see you make a fool of yourself either. No matter yesterday, you're in favour today.''

''So there's a good side to this?'' she challenged him sarcastically.

''Shh, they're coming,'' he warned as though the distant figures could hear every word. ''We're love birds remember? You've got a minute to give me your answer.''

''Oh my God, it's *no*.'' She waved to the approaching figures. They waved back. ''I can't, Ashe.''

He liked the way she said his name. It lingered in the air between them, curiously like an endearment. ''It could mean a great deal. Nic is taking life too hard.''

She met his gaze briefly. This man was a hypnotist. Not only that, he was succeeding in banishing Josh from her mind. "For all you know I might be terrible with children."

"No, you're good with them," he contradicted her. "You'll have plenty of help. I have a housekeeper. She has staff. I'm not panting for wild sex if that's what you're worrying about."

"Far from it," she said tartly, keeping her gaze firmly on her bare toes. Wild sex! The very thought made a blinding white light snap on inside her.

"Time's up, Christy," he said, aware of the delicate natural fragrance she gave off like a flower. He wanted her. He wanted her so badly it astonished him. And he wasn't a man to waste time.

"It's blackmail, you know." She surrendered. God knows why.

His dark eyes gleamed. "You're thinking of someone else. Not me."

The children ran to them excitedly, sunny smiles, cheeks rosy with warmth and exercise.

"Hello, beautiful!" Ashe pulled Katey down onto the sand beside him. "Enjoy your walk?"

Christy just had time to stare briefly at the cloudless blue heavens before Kit landed in

her lap, dark curls clustering around his an-
gelic little face.

What have I done? she thought.

What have I done?

CHAPTER FOUR

Two weeks later, Christy, a child on each hand, stood in front of Augusta Downs homestead, staring up at the wonderfully pleasing facade wondering how the early pioneers had ever succeeded in their undertaking of reproducing "Home" in the overwhelming vastness and isolation of the Australian Outback, with its heat and blazing colours and the crippling seasons of drought. Augusta, a homestead with its bore-watered home gardens and myriad outbuildings seen from the ground, created the fleeting illusion of an English country estate, emphasizing the importance of the English, Irish and Scottish families in the pioneering annals of the nation. Seen from the air, Augusta, showplace of the McKinnon operation, presented an awesome sight; a settlement like a small township set down in a vast riverine desert with blood-red soil, rolling red dunes, gatherings of great gums along the lagoons and billabongs, dead desert oaks bleached bone-white by a scorching sun on the ancient level plains, no other human habitation to the shimmering, mirage bedevilled horizon.

In such a place as starkly different to the British Isles as it could possibly be, the transported McKinnon family had lived and died. Here, too, they had developed their great selection without pause since it was taken up in the mid 1800s and named Augusta Downs after the bride of the first immigrant adventurer, James Andrew McKinnon.

At barely twenty-one, with the financial assistance of his well-to-do family in Scotland, he'd been able to purchase a great holding, he and others; a very special breed of men, the forerunners of the great cattle kings. James' driving ambition was to breed great herds of beef cattle, in the process founding his own dynasty in this new Promised Land. His extraordinary life one of unremitting hardships, self-denial and indomitable vision paid off handsomely, if not for him then for his descendants.

Eventually James had persuaded two of his brothers, Duncan and William to join him. At first the brothers worked Augusta, then as James began to extend the family holdings to the north and east Duncan and William took over the running of the new McKinnon out-posts. Today the total holdings through the gi-ant State of Queensland and the Northern Territory itself twice the size of Texas but with about one per cent of the Texan population, covered an area greater than the size of the McKinnon's native Scotland. In the vast Outback where the pioneering deeds of ex-traordinary daring do were commonplace, the kings of the cattle country had forged their own special mystique. Fascinating and roman-tic to the city dwellers, the life was not without its ruinous conditions and the constant dangers of isolation. Cattlemen had to be tough. Cattlemen let nothing stand in their way. Small wonder Ashe McKinnon had swept her off her feet with his sheer audaciousness, Christy thought.

She knew already Augusta remained the family flagship, the jewel in the crown to this day. The homestead, she realised as she stud-ied it, had been added to greatly over the years, obviously to accommodate the growing family. What looked like the original gabled two-storied building, now the central section, with-out the usual colonial verandahs, had sprouted huge symmetrical wings probably by the turn of the century with the balconics, verandahs, slender pillars and decorative cast-iron balustrades that made it so very picturesque.

"Can we go inside, please, Christy?" Kit piped up, jerking Christy out of her reverie. "I want a drink."

"Of course, darling." She bent to him remorsefully. He had been so very good right throughout the long flight to Longreach where a charter flight stood by to wing them into Augusta Downs. Ashe had intended to fly them himself but something unforeseen had cropped up. Something to do with drilling difficulties associated with sinking a huge bore.

"I'm so sorry, Kit," Christy apologised. "I was busy admiring the homestead."

"It's lovely isn't it?" Katey beamed with pleasure. Despite all the travel she was still full of beans. "This is the McKinnon ancestral home. Uncle Ashe said it belongs to us all. It doesn't really," she confided to Christy, rolling her eyes drolly. "Uncle Ashe is the real owner, but we're his family."

"He certainly loves you," Christy said as though it was something she had just discovered. At least something she hadn't glimpsed at the wedding.

Inside the grandly furnished homestead—Christy didn't know where to look first—Mrs. Davidson, the housekeeper who only answered to Lonnie—later on Christy learned Lonnie had been christened Leonora by her opera-buff mother, a name that clearly didn't suit—bustled around in an all-out effort to make them welcome and comfortable. Their luggage had already been placed in their rooms by the attractive young station hand, Garry, who had been allotted the job of driving them up from the landing strip to the house, close on fifteen minutes away. Their bedrooms in the west wing all adjoined except for Christy's sitting room, which acted as a buffer. It was a lovely mellow feminine place of satin and rosy chintz sofas, with books, a very interesting series of watercolour paintings on the walls, a cylinder front desk with beautiful brass fittings, paired with an antique chair and a broad view of the extraordinary landscape.

''Now young Kit,'' Lonnie spoke to the little boy who was openly yawning. ''You can either have a bedroom to yourself or share with Katey. As you can see, Miss—'' Lonnie turned to address Christy now.

''Oh please, *Christy*—'' Christy insisted.

Lonnie showed her pleasure, her mouth curling up in a smile. "As you can see, Christy, Mr. Ashe had a second bed brought in just in case."

"In case of what?" Kit demanded.

Christy tousled his hair. "In case you're lonely. The room can certainly take two beds and then some." The bedrooms were huge by today's standards. "And those beautiful embroidered linens?" she queried, thinking them perhaps too delicate and expensive for the children.

"Must use them, Christy," Lonnie assured her. "There are crates and crates of things in this house—wedding presents from way back that have never been opened."

"Good grief!" Christy bent to hug Kit who nuzzled her neck, obviously missing his mother.

"You have to see it to believe it," Lonnie clucked. "They really want opening up, but Mr. Ashe won't give the okay to do it. A lot of it was his parents' stuff."

And he isn't ready for it, Christy thought, releasing Kit who ran off with his sister to make a tour of their rooms.

"I want to share," Kit told Christy when they returned. "Last time I was here I was little."

"Nearly a year ago, pet." Lonnie lay an affectionate hand over his shoulder. "Don't you remember the whole McKinnon clan turned up for Christmas?"

"It was wonderful!" Katey plonked herself down on the long bench upholstered with beautiful needlepoint tapestry at the foot of Christy's huge canopy bed. The bed, which was easily bigger than king size, could accommodate a family. "Uncle Ashe puts up a great big Christmas tree in the front hall," Katey told her. "It's huge and it has wonderful ornaments all over it. Some of them are very old and very precious, a big star at the top, and tons of presents for everyone under the tree. Mummy was expecting our little baby then, but it died."

Christy went to the child and sat down beside her. "Part of us never dies, Katey. The important part, the soul. While we're enjoying this lovely holiday with Uncle Ashe your little sister, I know she was named Elizabeth after your grandmother, is having a glorious time in

Heaven. There's no sickness or unhappiness there. God doesn't allow it.''

"I still wish she was here," Katey insisted, looking sad.

Christy held her. ''Of course you do, so you can really love her, but she's watching you.''

"That's what Mummy says," Katey confided. "Then she cries.''

"It's the saddest experience in the world, Katey, for a mother to part with her child. Try to think of it as a separation but not forever. You and Kit are a great comfort and joy to Mummy and Daddy. They adore you.''

"But we're going to leave them one day when we get married," Kit pointed out, sounding older than his years.

"Don't be silly. No one will marry you. You're way too little," Katey scoffed.

"I mean when I grow up," Kit retorted.

"When you grow up, Kit, you're going to be very, very handsome," Christy said, drawing him to her and examining his face. "You're tired. I think you should have forty winks after we decide on the beds. Come on, let's have a look at the room.

"So which is it to be?" Christy said when they reached Katey's bedroom. "Seeing this is

Katey's room she really should have first pick.''

''Okay then...'' Katey eyed the beds then the room. ''I want this one.'' She went to the bed nearest the verandah, which looked like it could have been slept in by Queen Victoria. ''I love the yellow bedspread. Is the other one right for you, Kit?''

''Boys don't have pink.'' Kit pulled a dubious grimace.

''We can change the coverlet easily,'' Lonnie assured him in her easy, comfortable way, her warm brown eyes magnified by her specs. ''I have a very nice blue one in mind.''

''Anyway I'm the nearest to Christy's room,'' Kit said, making it sound for all the world he'd be nearest to heaven.

''When he has bad dreams, he cries,'' Katey told her, mildly scornful.

Immediately Kit looked down, his long eyelashes languishing on his satiny cheeks.

''He won't cry when I tuck him in,'' Christy promised. ''We're going to have such a good time during the day both of you are going to fall asleep as soon as your heads hit the pillow. And *stay* asleep.''

''Will you listen for me, Christy? Don't shut the door,'' Kit asked, anxiety in his sapphire eyes.

''I'll never be asleep so deeply I won't hear you, darling,'' Christy said and vowed there and then to keep an eye and ear open. ''I won't shut the door either.''

It had taken some convincing for Nicole to agree to this time apart from her children. On the one hand it was obvious even to Nicole she was desperately in need of time out with her husband, but being such a devoted mother she had been seriously concerned by the idea of leaving the two young ones. She had never done so before. Only the fact Nicole held Ashe in the highest esteem and had taken such an instant liking to Christy had the matter been settled at all. This put great responsibility on Christy but it also brought into play her organizational skills and the deep maternal feelings she now knew were in her.

Christy put an arm around each child; touched and grateful, both of them melted into her. ''This is going to be a lovely holiday. It's my first time and the two of you are going to show me everything.''

And so it was the three-week holiday on Augusta began. A time that was destined to totally change lives.

While the children went with Lonnie for homemade lemonade, Christy saw Garry off. "Maybe you and I could go riding one day?" Garry suggested, hooking one high-heeled riding boot around a verandah chair. "What'd ya say?"

"At this stage, Garry—" she smiled, not wanting to be unfriendly even if he was being forward "—I'd say no."

"I won't give up." He smiled cheekily back into her eyes. "You just might change your mind."

"That might well be," she answered, somewhere between polite and blithe.

"'Course you're a guest of the Boss." The thought seemed to dissolve a lot of Garry's initial enthusiasm. "I might have to ask his permission."

"Really?" Christy's face reflected her surprise.

"Hell, yes." Garry nodded emphatically. "Don't give me that big-eyed look. The Boss can get really stroppy if anyone steps out of line. Every guy on the station knows they have to be very careful with the ladies.''

She nearly laughed. ''You mean you can't give in to impulses like inviting the house guests out riding?''

''Something like that.'' He grinned, showing excellent teeth. ''I might get sacked.''

''So apparently you've taken a risk?''

''Why not?'' he asked firmly. ''I've never seen such a beautiful girl in my life.''

''Imagine!'' Christy narrowed her eyes against the brilliant glare. ''Unless I'm mistaken, here's the Boss now.''

''Is, too.'' Garry straightened instantly. ''I'd better get cracking.'' He loped off the verandah. ''See ya, Christy.''

Despite his bravado Garry lost no time in drawing away, putting one arm out the window to acknowledge Ashe.

He didn't get a return wave, Christy noticed. She remained where she was while Ashe brought the open Jeep to a halt at the base of the steps.

''Hi!'' His smile lifted the handsome severity of his expression to a flash of radiance. ''I've had to leave them to it,'' he explained.

"I was more concerned about how you and the kids survived all the travel?"

"It was well worth it for all of us," Christy said with pleasure, unable to control the involuntary rippling thrills the sight of him gave her. He held his six-foot-three frame with such arrogant male grace, like the hero of some adventure in the Outback commercial. She drank in the pearl-grey akubra he now swept off, his hair tousled into crisp curls, red bandanna, blue denim work shirt, fancy buckled silver belt, fitted jeans, high-heeled riding boots that made him tower even taller.

"You should recognise me when you see me again." He moved towards her with a mocking smile and gave a little tug on a lock of her long blond hair.

"It's because you look so good." She tilted her head right back to look up at him. "I like the gear."

"We all wear pretty much the same thing around here," he replied smoothly.

"Some obviously better than others." Lanky, lean Garry, attractive as he was with sun-streaked hair and nut-brown eyes, didn't look anything like Ashe McKinnon.

"What was Garry doing here?" Ashe now asked, a little coolly, untying his red bandanna and stripping it off.

"He brought us up from the airstrip." Christy looked at him, trying to read his thoughts. "I thought you would know."

"His job was to bring you and the luggage. Take the luggage into the house. Not strike up a conversation, for God's sake."

Her eyes lit with a touch of defiance. "So much for democracy."

"Oh I'm very democratic," he said. "Only nothing happens on Augusta I don't want."

"I just hope I remember," Christy retorted dryly.

"If he's gone and asked you to go riding with him, that's never going to happen," Ashe warned.

"Well not this weekend," Christy tossed off mock-sweetly. "Have you come home for lunch?" She hoped he was going to say yes.

"Hmm," he said, eyeing her steadily. Neat little violet top, very feminine and sexy, skinny-legged, bright blue jeans. Her golden-blond hair hung richly around her face and flowed over her shoulders, the green eyes and creamy complexion were as fresh as spring.

"I can't say I blame Garry for momentarily going crazy." Irritation gave way to a wry understanding. "I had to come myself to check if you were as beautiful as I last saw you or you'd wilted away in the heat."

"What heat?" Christy ran her hand up under her nape. It was damp but she didn't tell him. "Shall we go inside?" she asked. He was making her feel too much a woman. "The children will be thrilled you're here."

"And what about you?" He lay a light staying hand on her shoulder.

"I'm still trying to figure out how I agreed to come out here," she confessed, "to a complete and utter stranger. I'm not normally a reckless person."

"Come on," he jeered. "Anyway you did it for Nic and Brendan."

"For their sakes, yes." Her pose was casual. Inside she felt electric. "You have the most wonderful private kingdom. I can't wait to explore it."

"I'm glad you like it," he returned, still lazily studying her.

"Just so long as I don't have to drop a curtsey at your approach."

"No one around here does that," he assured her, "but if you ever feel inclined…!"

Lonnie lost no time putting the lunch on the table, a deep-dish chicken pie with little herb-and-sausage flavoured dumplings which tempted the children, served with a salad, and for afterwards, caramel ice-cream topped with ginger syrup, which the children pronounced so "yummy" Christy had to have some.

Happy, content and drowsy, both agreed without a murmur to an afternoon siesta while Ashe showed Christy over the house. She'd known at first glance it was furnished in a variety of styles, English, French, Oriental, all the rooms down to the guest bedrooms were filled with art and antiques the family had collected over the generations. To Christy's fascinated eyes it was a veritable Aladdin's cave.

She found very entertaining, Ashe's running commentary. It was full of interest, very informative, sometimes revealing and delivered with panache. This was a man who had lived all his life in what was without question a grand house without he or the house being in any way grandiose. No matter the sheer size, and they didn't cover the entire house, Augusta homestead was none the less very much a home where the one family had lived, loved and died, each generation leaving their mark and all kinds of collections.

"My grandfather left this particular collection to me." They were in Ashe's study with beautiful cedar wood panelling and hung with a collection of equestrian paintings and a glass display case filled with sculptures of horses right through the ages.

"Those are Tang." Ashe pointed to a shelf where several proud and sturdy pottery horses in coloured glazes rested.

"I particularly love the one with the rider," Christy said.

"Here, have a closer look," Ashe offered, going to pick up the beautiful little model.

"Oh no, I'd feel frightful if anything went wrong."

He clicked his tongue. "It's not going to go wrong. You love horses."

"I do." Christy took the pottery figure carefully into her hands, admiring the vigour of the sculpture. "It appears to be a different horse from the one beside it," she remarked. "The other has a broader neck. It's taller and more muscular as well. A different breed?"

"Well observed, Miss Parker," he congratulated her. "Although they're both Tang Dynasty and well over thirteen or fourteen hundred years old, the second horse belongs to a breed imported from the West. The little man standing beside the horse is—"

"His groom of course," Christy said in delight. "The glazes on both are beautiful. I feel honoured you've shown me." Christy extended her glazed pottery figure to Ashe who returned it to the cabinet.

"We used to have a pottery horse with a marvellous head from the Han Dynasty. Goodness knows what happened to it. I hate to say it but some guest in the house must have taken a fancy to it."

"Obviously you mean it was stolen?"

"Of course. I loved it when I was a boy. You could see the nostrils actually trembling. A Bachtrian pony descended from the Perso-Arab horses brought into China to serve to cavalry."

"So horses are a McKinnon passion?"

"Very much so. The bronzes are very fine. That particular one is by Degas. Many of the equestrienne paintings are nineteenth-century French. My great-grandmother, Celeste, had a passion for the Oriental school of artists as you can see by the large painting over the mantel. You probably know the Orientals flourished in Europe toward the end of the last century. Grandmere Celeste, she was French by the way, a McKinnon family connection, found the paintings very thrilling and romantic.''

''I'm not surprised. That one is marvellous,'' Christy said. It was a scene where a magnificent pure white Arabian horse was being offered for sale in a North African bazaar with all its attendant tumultuous colours and exotica. ''You must be very proud of your home and your heritage.''

He met her gaze. ''Well it's the story of frontier Australia, isn't it? The history and development of a great pastoral industry as well as a rich social history. If you're interested we have a great deal of archival material in the family library. We'll go there now. There are personal accounts of both my family's lives and the intertwining lives of our neighbours even though they might have been hundreds of miles away. My aunt Zoe—she holds a Doctorate of Philosophy—has published three books in connection with our cultural heritage. She's working on another now. You'll like her.

Zoe is a very clever and interesting woman. She also manages to combine her considerable academic knowledge with a great sense of fun.''

Incredulously she heard his words. ''I'm going to meet her?''

''Sure,'' he told her crisply. ''Sometime.''

''You sound very certain.'' She was shaken to her toes by the intensity of his expression.

''Don't panic. I'm not going to hold you prisoner.'' His brilliant gaze, the distillation of a passionate nature, ran over her.

''That's good because I know you could if you wanted to.''

''Come on, Christy,'' he said with surprising gentleness. ''You know you're keen to be my friend.''

She half turned, redirecting her gaze. ''You're far too uncomfortable for that.''

''*Uncomfortable,*'' he scoffed. ''Now I know where I stand.''

''You know what I mean.'' She turned back with the challenge, ''You darn near held me to ransom.''

''How so?'' His black eyes, so deep, so beautiful, were impossible to read.

"I still don't believe you trust me." Why would he?

"I haven't trusted women for many many years." His vibrant voice, though mocking, was a touch bitter. "To illustrate a point. Not so very long ago, a matter of weeks, you were on the edge of upstaging my cousin's wedding."

"I wasn't." She held to the fine edge of control.

"You were where you *weren't* supposed to be," he pointed out.

"I did nothing illegal."

"Not socially acceptable, Christy," he said in a low, ironic tone. "At that same reception my cousin's brand-new husband was using his strength to pull you into his arms. I recall the moment as vividly as though it happened this very morning."

"Then I hope you noted I was fending him off?" Christy was shocked by a sudden urge to hit him. Hell, he had no hesitation about hurting her.

"Oddly I didn't," he clipped off. "I was too busy paying close attention to Deakin."

She was aware of the ambivalence in their feelings for each other, a strong attraction, a threat of hostility. "I'm sorry about all of it. I must have been temporarily out of my mind."

"You'd have to be to want to ruin a wedding."

"What I wanted was to give Josh a good fright. I thought he *loved* me." She despised the residual emotion in her own voice. "I still can't believe the way he acted."

"So your feelings for him haven't evaporated?" He sounded distant and very direct at the same time.

"Why don't you try to understand" She stared up at him, in a conflicting maze of emotion. "What if someone had done the same thing to *you?* Answer *that,* Ashe McKinnon." Little flames lit Christy's eyes. "I bet you've got a ferocious temper."

"Which I mostly keep well under control. Right now I'm having trouble." He grasped her shoulders, his fingers exploring the delicate bones. What was passing between them was a difficult, dangerous current. He gave in to his desire, bringing his mouth down on hers, aching for it like some powerful drug, remembering the last time.

For Christy a whole range of emotions were fiercely transmitted. She felt the faint rasp of his skin as his mouth crushed her pulsing lips. His tongue engaged in a mad mating dance with hers, as his hands steadied her. It lasted only seconds yet it left her trembling, with no rules to follow. She had never encountered such sexual power. He was the best and the worst of men and he wasn't always kind.

"Why do you do this to us both?" Her powerful arousal made her angry. This was a man who fed on women's faithlessness.

"A summer storm," he said in a faultlessly cool way, easing one calloused finger over the tender pads of her lips. Like a baby's skin. Newly bared. "I'm a man. I have my wants."

"The truth is, you're mocking me. And you like it."

"Now there's an interesting spin." He observed her closely. "If I'm mocking you, Christy, I'm mocking myself."

"You can't keep on doing it," she said jaggedly. "I'm here to look after the children."

"You're also having a holiday. Believe it or not. I want you to enjoy yourself. You're here to spend time with the children, certainly. You're also here to spend some time with *me*."

She hardened her voice, her eyes darkening. "Ah, the authoritarian cattle baron. Could you possibly tell me in what special capacity?"

Just to confound her, he changed tack, exerting that unpredictable fantastic charm. "Not as my sleeping partner, unless it excites you."

The experience would electrify her. "I'm still grieving my own stupidity," she told him sharply.

"Then it shouldn't take long. I can't believe a man like Josh Deakin left any indelible mark on you. You've never really loved *anyone*."

"What about my mother and father?"

"Any *man*, I mean. I know you love your mother and father. But you're a big girl now. I'm talking men. Passion. A lot of people believe romantic love is myth. Nothing more than illusion. It exists only for a short time before it fizzles out. I forget the name of the guy who wrote a book about that."

Christy made a little dismissive sound. "I don't buy the argument. The bloom of romance has never faded for my parents."

"Then they're very lucky. I'm equally certain they work at keeping their love alive?"

Christy surrended to her musings. "Yes they do. They nurture one another. However,

I think *you,* like your guru, have probably gone sour on life.''

''So why the hell am I staring into your beautiful green eyes?''

''You just like playing with fire,'' she told him acidly, riding high on the emotion generated by his kiss.

He shook his head. ''A man could get trapped that way. I'm going through a period when I'm considering a good working strategy for marriage.''

His eyes were full on hers. ''Don't look at me.'' She gave a little shiver. ''I still believe in love.''

''A lot of people who fall in love and get married finish up desperate to escape. Sooner or later reality intrudes. Falling in love isn't loving, Christy. That's a misconception, as you've found out to your cost. There must be the right way of going about it to make love happen. The same interests, the same values, the same goals.''

''I could never get married without being in love,'' Christy maintained, when her ''love'' for Josh was little more than a sham.

''Love as in lust? Perhaps a little more elegant than that.''

"A heck of a lot more elegant as you put it." He was disturbing her terribly.

"Plans. Flowers. Church. Reception. A solemn and important occasion. Women revel in it like their wedding day is going to last the rest of their lives. A man just gets through it."

"You're having me on?" Temper rare in her sparked.

"That, as well," he suddenly relented. "Anyway why get so defensive? That kiss we just shared was quite feverish, I thought. Almost romantic passion. Certainly sexual attraction. The tricks our hormones play to hoodwink us."

"You terrify me, Ashe McKinnon," she said, inhaling deeply.

"I mean to, Christy." His tone was an unnerving balance between tender and sarcastic. "No, I'm fooling. My work is my life. I might be the top gun but I have a family to answer to. Lots of McKinnon money has been put into my hands."

"So there's really only one thing remaining?" Delicately she raised her brows. "You'll have to take a wife."

"Wife. Mother." His handsome mouth pursed. "Someone very, very real. Young, reasonably good-looking—plain simply won't do—intelligent, warm, trustworthy, responsible—''

''You seem to have everything in order. Anything else?''

''I haven't finished yet.'' He looked into her face, black eyes tauntingly bright. ''Strong. A person in her own right. A woman who could easily become a director, sit on the board of McKinnon Enterprises. It would be an enormous plus if she were also great in bed.''

''Isn't it a mercy I might fail you there,'' Christy snapped.

He met that with a low, unsettling laugh. ''I daresay we could always find out. But all in good time? I wouldn't want you to feel any anxiety about leaving your bedroom door unlocked.'' He lowered his right hand to the curve of her jaw and cupped it with his long fingers. ''Let's continue on our tour of exploration, shall we?''

''The house?'' Christy tried to block off all emotion.

''Of course the house,'' he smoothly replied.

*   *   *

The library was very handsome indeed with a series of magnificent bookcases set in arcaded recesses all around the room. The leather bindings of the books glowed richly; ruby, emerald, olive, dark yellow, burgundy and browns, with titles and accents in gleaming gold. There were an extraordinary number of volumes of all sizes, some with elaborate bindings like vellum, velvet and silk. Deep armchairs were set all around the room with small easily moveable tables nearby. A Regency library table holding a large pewter vase filled with pink and cream roses was placed in the centre of the room, directly beneath a massive multi-armed bronze dore chandelier. A beautiful Persian rug, predominantly ruby, covered most of the gleaming timber floor, muffling their footsteps as they walked in.

Christy who loved books was immediately spellbound. This was a place of quiet and contemplation with the dignity and beauty of another era. Quite obviously the McKinnons had been men and women of education and exceptional intelligence. Every part of the house, not just the magnificent library, spoke of the broad scope of their interests.

Ashe studied her rapt face as she proceeded to circle the room staring up at the bookcases and their contents.

"Surely this must be one of the finest private libraries in the country," she asked without turning her blond head. "Few people could own such a large and comprehensive library let alone house all these books."

"As a matter of fact it is. With forms of entertainments so limited, small wonder the people of the Outback are great readers. And collectors. My great-grandfather had a taste for discovery and exploration. Natural history, that kind of thing. The bookcase where you're in front of now holds some rare works."

"Marvellous," she breathed. "I majored in journalism for my Arts Degree. I spent two years with *Impact* magazine. I love books."

"I can see that." He smiled. "You're welcome to browse anytime."

"Could I take a volume up to my room?" She turned to ask, her face vivid with interest.

"Certainly. I know you would care for it."

"And who is this gentleman here?" She gazed at a handsome uniformed officer of perhaps the early nineteenth century.

"An ancestor," Ashe said. "He was killed in the battle of Waterloo."

"How unfortunate. He was so young."

"There were other McKinnons killed young," he replied a little bleakly. "One in a massacre. I won't go into the details. Four from two world wars. There are more portraits in the next room. The family still calls it the smoking room where the gentlemen used to retire, but smoking is taboo these days. It's more like a trophy room, artefacts, et cetera, brought back by various members of the family from overseas trips."

He allowed her to precede him into the room. "Some of the stuff is quite bizarre. A great-uncle was obsessed with all things Egyptian. Another with all things Oriental, yet another adored India. Just a moment I'll turn on the light. Lonnie has drawn the curtains."

Above the richly carved black marble fireplace was a portrait of a very handsome man of middle years who could only be Ashe McKinnon's father, the resemblance was so strong. What distinguished father from son was the colour of the eyes. Ashe McKinnon's eyes were so darkly brilliant they were almost black. His father's eyes, which appeared to follow one around the room, were notably blue. So where had those dark eyes come from? Ashe's mother? The mother he never talked about?

"What a wonderfully handsome and distinguished man," Christy said, noting sadly for all his handsomeness the man in the painting did not have his son's tremendous...Christy could only think of one word...*dash*. Or even that high-mettled look that made Ashe McKinnon appear so blazingly alive.

"What a sad day it must have been when your father and your uncle were killed," she said, voice faltering.

"The worst day of my life."

"Worse than when your mother left?" she asked gently.

"I was a child when my mother left," he reminded her, his face assuming its closed expression. "I felt as a child. I was a grown man when I had to contend with my father's death and my uncle's. They weren't only brothers, they were very, very close. Family and business partners. That's why I watch over Mercedes and Callista."

"Would you be very angry if I asked where you got your dark eyes?" Brilliant jet and very deep.

"You want to know everything," he responded with a slight edge. "My mother was amazingly beautiful, as you are. And she had ravishing colouring. Blond hair and dark eyes. A combination one doesn't see very often. She had Italian blood in her. My eyes are said to be like hers but darker. Satisfied?"

"It's a normal question, Ashe. Your response isn't. You don't have to have me decapitated."

"I'm light-years away from wanting to do that," he said, his voice unbearably ironic.

"Was there ever a portrait of your mother?" she felt compelled to ask.

He shrugged a powerful shoulder. "I wouldn't know where to find it."

"Okay, so it exists?"

"I hope you're not proposing to go in search of it."

"You need to talk about it, Ashe," she said, studying his face.

"Don't be absurd. My mother went out of my life over twenty years ago. As simple as that."

"What was her name?"

"You're extremely inquisitive."

"And you're on the brink of open hostility." She spoke calmly. "I can see it in your eyes. I just wanted to know a little about your life, that's all. Yours is an astonishing one so different from my own. You belong here in this incredible world with a mansion for a homestead and the wild desert heartland on your doorstep. It's so exotic and romantic. It really is!"

"You're coming in from the outside, Christy," he pointed out. "It's unrelenting hard work."

"But you love it, don't you?"

"It's my life," he answered simply.

It was what made him so powerful and strong. "There are so many photographs on the wall of the sitting room you've given me," she said. "I'm longing to have a good look at them. To see the way you grew up. I thought there might be one of you with your parents?"

His laugh was brief. "Sorry, Christy, you'll look in vain. If you're sweetly imagining I might want to move back into my mother's life again, you couldn't be more wrong."

"That's sad."

"It was, but that was many long years ago."

"So she just went away?" She thought of how it would feel for father and son.

"Well she did leave a few clues," he replied. "Christy, do you mind if we get off this? No one has mentioned my mother for a very long time. I'd like to keep it that way."

"I'm sorry," she apologised. "I'm not just being curious. I'm really interested." She gazed around her. "You know this would be a great setting for a book."

"So long as you don't make me one of your central characters."

"I've always wanted to write," she confided.

"Why don't you then?"

"I've been too busy making a living," she said simply. "I wasn't born with a silver spoon in my mouth. I need my pay cheque to get by."

"But you do have the will to succeed?"

"I do." Her answer was emphatic.

"And you're not looking for a wealthy candidate to marry?"

"You mean like Josh." She spoke a little angrily.

"Josh," he answered curtly, "is in for one very big surprise if he thinks Callista is going to be open-handed with her money. She has a very good business head on her shoulders, which she was probably at pains to hide from Deakin in the first flush of their romance. Besides, *I* manage most of Mercedes and Callista's assets, which include grazing properties in the McKinnon chain."

"I just can't imagine all that money." She shrugged. "I read once an Australian heiress said it's just as stressful to have too much money as no money."

He laughed, his dark eyes trained on her. "It doesn't work for playboys. Or playgirls for that matter. As for me, I'm too busy."

"Maybe you're pleasure deprived," she suggested. "Maybe that's what wrong with you. Maybe that's why you're thinking on lines of marriage strategies. That's it! It just hit me. You haven't got time to fit love into your life."

"But the love of a good woman could save me?" He made her stop her circling to face him.

"Hopefully. You're way too cynical. And I don't like the way you look down that straight nose at me. I know we got off on the wrong foot.''

''Hell, yes,'' he admitted, ''but it wasn't all bad. How do you know I didn't want you from the first moment I laid eyes on you? How do you know, for that matter, you aren't the woman who started me on thinking marriage contracts?''

She had to steady herself. ''I would never be so desperate as to enter into a loveless marriage contract. It would be like going to prison. You're too complex a man, Ashe. Too brooding.''

''But I make your hands shake.''

She found herself holding them up. ''You spook me.''

''Now that's some piece of information.'' He captured those hands. Staring down at her ringless fingers. ''A very pretty hand,'' he remarked. ''So much for a woman's talk. You should wear a flawless, Colombian emerald, flanked by diamonds. You could draw your hair back and wear the earrings to match. A chignon. Isn't that what you call it? A difficult style for a woman without beautiful features.''

"What are you talking about, Ashe?" Christy stammered. Something about him triggered shock and alarm.

"I'm not sure," he bit off. "Do you want me to read your palm?"

Excitement jetted like a fountain. Excitement difficult to endure and very hard to construe. Ashe McKinnon had great passion in him. She knew that. But maybe not the capacity to love. An affliction based on grief from the past.

"I'm an open book," she told him, too intensely. The current that was running between them had her quaking.

"No, you're not," he contradicted. "You're too fascinating."

"Give me back my hand." This man was a devil.

He stared at her and saw she was perturbed. "Of course. Sometimes you're so cool, other times vulnerable. I expect it's because you're recovering from a broken romance and all. Just a little warning, Christy. Don't try to understand me. I don't understand myself."

CHAPTER FIVE

MORNING broke over the Timeless Land; the great shimmering desert that was the oldest part of the earth's crust.

Birdsong rang out to welcome the sun, its power and brilliance resonating away to the horizons; trillions of birds uncaging their hearts. The illuminated sky, the silvery-grey of a pearl, was spread with colours that intensified by the minute; pink, mauve, rose, violet, yellow, streaks of fiery red. All awaiting the sun to turn everything to such a density of blue just looking up made one feel very close to Heaven.

Christy's dreams had been going around in circles. Ashe was in every one and she no longer wondered why. Most mornings she woke to the sounds of a quiet suburban jungle, now she was roused by an avalanche of musical sound; sweet, piercing, warbling, sobbing, the mad gurgling cackle of the kookaburras, one of her most nostalgic childhood memories; a glorious cacophony of sound, so different from what she was used to, for a moment she wasn't sure where she was, or even if she was in the middle of a fantasy. She had never slept in a huge canopied bed. Never possessed such exquisite bed linens. And the sound outside...

Christy threw back the light coverlet and padded out onto the verandah. Fragrance was all around her, its softness, freshness, gorgeous boronia, overwhelmingly close. An abundance of scents. She couldn't possibly track them. She stared out over the great gums that extended their long arms over massed lilies that grew at their feet. She felt flooded with pleasure.

This was the desert. The wild heart. Yet strangely trees and vegetation flourished. It wasn't a desert at all but a place of wonder. She drew in deep lungfuls of the marvellous air like it was some miraculous medication that could offer eternal life. Christy the nature lover, one hand to her breast, her eyes closed, was experiencing a feeling close to ecstasy. Her blood pulsed through her veins. Her soul rose up on wings. Lifted to the skies...

The sun at the horizon was swiftly rising in an incandescent golden arc. Christy could feel its brilliance and heat through her shut eyelids. She thought of the ancients, the aboriginal tribes who understood and worshipped nature. These were the people most likely to die if they were ever locked up. This beautiful morning she felt a great connection...a great understanding...a white woman's Dreaming.

"That's it, hold it. I really need a camera."

A man's vibrant voice thoroughly roused her. Christy opened her eyes, blinking rapidly. There was too much within her heart to feel any trace of embarrassment.

"Is it some kind of dawn worship?" Ashe asked.

She leaned right over the balustrade. "Ashe?" Of course it was Ashe. No one else had his alluring voice with all the taunting, teasing, downright sarcastic inflections.

"You mean you were expecting someone else?" His dark head dropped back the better to see her. "Rapunzel, Rapunzel, let down your hair. That's quite a cascade!"

"You surely don't intend climbing up?" A wild clamour peaked in her. Why wouldn't he? He was that daring.

"Like to see me?" he scoffed.

She laughed, uncertain he was serious. "You're joking of course?"

"No. I seem to be becoming less and less inhibited around you."

To increase her extraordinary sense of exhilaration, he strode from his position on the grass directly below her to a spot further up where a vigorously glossy leaved creeper thickly covered the stonewall.

Did he really intend to climb it? Going on what she had learned about him, the answer was yes. Christy flew back into her bedroom and pulled on her pale pink satin robe. She quickly belted it then rushed back onto the verandah already stirred up, unnerved and curiously delighted.

"I think I deserve something for that." He looked so blazingly handsome and vital; swinging one long leg over the balustrade it would have tested any woman's virtue. "Now that's a very classy robe, Christy." He came towards her in his dashing cattleman's gear, brilliant eyes moving over her.

"I'm glad you like it." She told herself to stay calm. A very tall order with this disturbing man. Why hadn't some enterprising woman bedazzled him into marrying her?

"It's gorgeous and so are you," he drawled. "I'm sufficiently susceptible to a woman's beauty to find a nightie very appealing. It's not every woman, either, who can look ethereal first thing in the morning." His gaze slid with lazy admiration over the long blond flow of her hair, the green of her eyes, the sheen of her robe, the swell of her breasts.

Sparks of electricity tingled over her. "I never expected company, but life is full of surprises."

"Isn't it ever! This could well be the thrilling highlight of my day seeing you in a pearl pink satin nightgown out on the verandah, worshipping the rising sun."

"It was the birds. They woke me." Even as she spoke a flock of sulphur-crested cockatoos exploded from the red gums like a great burst of flowers.

"The Outback is famous for its birds and its early morning symphonies," Ashe said. "I accept your exultation. They've been known to affect me the same way. Aside from that, I expect you wanted to catch me before I left for the day?"

She suddenly saw that was so. But she denied it. "Nothing so planned. I swear I never thought of you for a minute."

"Then you force me to make a play for your attention." He stared down on her, giving every indication of being absorbed. "Good morning, Christine." He gave her name full resonance. "I hope you slept well?"

"Like a child. Don't do it, Ashe," she begged.

"But I want to kiss you. A kiss. Nothing more. I'm not about to tumble you into bed."

"I *know* that." She blushed, her heart skipping several beats as he put his hand beneath her chin.

"You're beautiful. Your hair shines like a halo."

He amazed her. Utterly amazed her. He shouldn't be seducing her this effortlessly. But it so excited her. Waves of sensation rose then spilled back through her body. Her sensitive nipples puckered with arousal. His mouth covered hers with the most exquisite voluptuousness. It was like he was peeling her clothes off, laying her skin bare to the cool morning air. It wasn't only dangerous. It was crazy. Possibly the start of a life-changing direction.

He must have thought so, too. "Can't overdo it," he murmured, slowly withdrawing his mouth from hers. "Taste testing. You taste like wild peaches."

It was an agony of delight, his pushing the boundaries. "You're having a great time, aren't you? Don't you think I know," Christy accused him.

"My marriage strategy, what else?" He half smiled at her, fingering a long strand of her hair. "You're an angel and I'm still marvelling. Your mother should have called you Angelica."

"I'm glad she didn't. I love Christy."

"In short you love love?"

"And you're afraid of it, Ashe McKinnon," she told him quietly. "Afraid of your own heart."

His expression turned purely sarcastic. "Sweet Christy, that's a line from a soap opera. I can't stand it. I was going to limit myself to one kiss but I think as a punishment I'll go for two."

Her green eyes fixed him with false warning. "I might scream."

"No you won't. I think you like a little suffering." This time he gathered her very closely into his arms, not anticipating a struggle and not getting one. He felt the crush of soft breasts against his hard chest. One of his strong arms was across her back; the other grasped a satin hip. The pressure of his kiss arched her neck. It hauled up raw emotions so deep within her it was as though they had existed in some secret cavern.

''I don't think you hate it so much,'' he mocked, when finally he raised his crow-black head. ''But you *can* apologise.''

''For what?'' It was difficult to find breath. The rasp of his darkly tanned polished skin chaffed her lips, not painfully, but erotically. Her whole body was literally quaking with excitement and confusion and the enormity of what was happening. Goodness knows what hungers, desires, this man could call up. Then she would really find out what it was like to have a broken heart.

''I think your credibility as a love-lorn jilted woman has been somewhat shattered,'' he offered a shade brutally.

''You surely don't think I thought you were being *kind* bringing me here?''

''You're the one who went into bat for romantic love, Christy,'' he reminded her. ''So much for your ex-lover.''

''I didn't say romantic love doesn't have its downside,'' she countered.

''Do you want him back?'' He turned her fully to face him.

Her heart contracted. For weeks now she had searched her heart, releasing memories she found were no longer painful. She hadn't known the *real* Josh at all.

''You don't even seem to miss him?''

She shook her head. ''No.''

It had come to her what she had felt for Josh was an illusion.

''You made a terrible mistake thinking you were in love with him,'' Ashe continued as if driven.

''Yes I did.'' She was calm with near despair. ''Satisfied, you cruel man?''

''For now.'' His hands circled her skin. ''But you're only on probation. We won't know for sure until you see him again. Most of the extended family usually come to me for Christmas.''

She gave a tiny moan. ''I'm not *family*. I won't be here.''

"You will," he said as though that was already settled. "Now I must go. I would have been gone ages ago except you did your level best to detain and distract me. See if you can work out a routine. One of Lonnie's girls will help you with the kids. Probably Meeta. She's good with children and she's very clever and artistic, as you'll find out. I want you to have time to yourself. You'll probably want to ride in the early morning, or late afternoon. Best to avoid the worst heat of the day. I've picked out a suitable mount I'm sure you'll like."

"Oh, thank you." She was so thrilled she reached out and curled her fingers around his arm.

"Enough of your little wiles!" he mocked, but his firm mouth softened momentarily.

"If you weren't being so damned nice I think I'd hate you," Christy said. "You wouldn't possibly have a well-schooled pony I could teach the children to ride? The earlier the better I always think. Both of them told me they've never been on a horse."

His dark eyes narrowed thoughtfully. "We didn't ask Nic but I'm sure she wouldn't mind. You're an accomplished rider. So *you say?*"

''Check me out for heaven's sake. I'm a good teacher, too.''

''And you're not crippled with false modesty. Give me today to straighten out a few problems. I've put a Jeep at your disposal. You and the kids can go for picnics, whatever. I'll leave it up to you.''

''Yes, Mr. McKinnon, sir.'' She touched her forehead with exquisite satire yet he gave her a lovely smile, a smile to die for.

''By the way, we're hosting a quartet of classical musicians at the weekend. For the last couple of years they've been coming Outback to bring the bush classical music.''

''But how marvellous!'' Christy was delighted.

''Think you could organise it?''

She was a little shaken, but excited. ''What? Organizing events is my forte. Who gets invited?''

''Everyone on the station,'' he said. ''As Augusta hosts it this year, quite a few from neighbouring stations will fly in. I've got a list. You can bet your life everyone will want to come.''

''So where is the concert to be held?'' Her voice showed her strong interest.

"In the Great Hall. That's where we usually hold our entertainments."

"Why not outdoors?" she suggested, visualizing the event in her mind. "Under the stars. The night sky is fantastic out here. No pollution to veil the brilliance of the stars."

"I hadn't thought of outside." He sounded a touch dubious.

"Let me think of it," Christy said. "I'll wander around the place—"

"Keep to the home compound."

It stopped just short of an order. "Right! I'll toss around a few ideas. Come up with something for you tonight. How does that sound?"

"It sounds very helpful," he told her with genuine relief. "I can't keep on cramming sixteen, seventeen hours into the one working day."

"So delegate, you poor man. Throw some of your workload at me. If I can't cut it you can always throw me out."

"That's not going to happen, Christy." Another powerful smile. She was starting to count them. "In all my years I can only remember one guest being turned off the property."

"So what did they do?" She turned up her face to ask. "Just so I'll know."

His mouth compressed. "A few objects from the house turned up in their luggage."

"Goodness! Do you mean to say you check?"

"Not in the ordinary course of events. The thefts would never have been discovered only the contents put too much of a strain on a piece of luggage. It burst open. Dare I add it was a woman journalist?"

She lifted her dimpled chin. "I didn't know your guests ran to journalists? Anyway your precious objects are safe with me."

"Of course I know that." He made a mock bow. "Now I'll take a short cut through your bedroom if you don't mind."

"I think I can cope with that." She was trying to keep her tone light but it came out sort of wavery, a dead give-away. "You can't take any more wall climbing?"

"Once was enough!" He twisted to look at her, blazingly alive, darkly handsome.

"It *was* pretty high."

He just smiled. "So I'll see you tonight." He crossed quietly to the door although the children's bedroom was a comfortable distance off. "I won't be able to get back to the house until sundown. We're sinking another bore, a steel-lined hole through black shale, mud rock and red and yellow clay, and we're still replacing drains with pipes. It costs tens of thousands of dollars but water is a miraculous resource out here."

"Isn't the Great Artesian Basin right under us?" she asked.

"It is. Under most of Queensland. It might be the world's largest underground source of fresh water, nearly nine billion megalitres, but too much of it is being wasted. There are hundreds of bores in our own State, the one with the most to gain and the most to lose, gushing precious water uncontrollably. The whole issue has to be seriously addressed. As vast as it is, the Basin is a finite resource."

"You're determined to stop the waste?" She glanced up, having moved with him to the door, and saw the committed look on his face.

"Absolutely. All open bore drains have to be capped. At the very least controlled by headworks."

"So why isn't everyone doing it?" She hadn't realised there was such a problem.

"Money, or lack of. It all comes down to cost. Many landowners back off because of the big drain on financial resources. Others concentrate on rehabilitation. All new bores have to be fully capped. Governments have to show the way. They have to fully support management plans and release the funds. As far as I'm concerned, it's dead simple. Our huge pastoral industry depends on the Basin. Without it Augusta and all the rest of the cattle and sheep stations in this State wouldn't be worth a cracker. The Basin has to be preserved for future generations."

"So it's a very big issue?" She decided there and then to check it all out.

He didn't have to think twice. "A solution *has* to be found. *Now*. Lecture over for the day," he assured her.

"No, I'm very interested. I'm going to find out a lot more."

"I didn't think you were just a pretty face." Before she could move—indeed all the time he was speaking she'd been rooted to the spot with attention—he dropped a brief near-affectionate kiss on her nose.

Even that she couldn't pass off lightly. After he had gone, Christy walked back to her bed and fell across it face down. What she felt for Ashe McKinnon was far too difficult to put into words. All she knew was the moment he came into her life she had changed immensely. She didn't function in the same way. It was even possible, and she had to face the truth, she had fallen crazily in love with him. She couldn't rule it out. Crazily in love with a man who talked strategies for marriage. Who wanted to banish romantic love for solid, feet-on-the-ground values? Tentatively she brought a hand up and touched the cushioned pads of her mouth. She thought she knew what a kiss was. She didn't. This was madness with the potential to cause heartbreak. But at least it was *her* secret.

The tiring effects of the children's long travels eventually caught up with them. They slept in until well after nine, only stirring when Christy came upstairs to check on them.

"Hey, you guys! Are you going to lie around in bed all day?" she asked playfully, standing at the bottom of Kit's bed and tickling his toes.

"What time is it, Christy?" Katey sat up, rubbing her nose.

"Well, not *that* late," Christy teased, glancing at her watch. "Nine-twenty, but you had a big day yesterday. Sleep well, poppet?" She turned to Kit, the nervous one.

"I can't believe it's morning." He pushed up from the bed then ran straight to Christy and hugged her around the middle. "I just closed my eyes."

"You've been asleep for hours and hours, silly," Katey groaned.

"So up you get!" Christy encouraged in a cheerful voice. "Lonnie is waiting to get your breakfast—anything you like outside of cake—then the three of us are going to tour the home compound."

"What's the home compound?" Kit asked excitedly, peering at Christy closely.

"The homestead and the stable complex and a few of the other buildings like the Great Hall," Katey, who was certainly going to lose a tooth, lisped.

Christy nodded. "I need the two of you to show me around. Musicians will be visiting the station this weekend with what's called a string quartet."

"Oh great!" Katey, who knew about orchestras, clapped her hands. "Is it nighttime? Will we be able to stay up?"

"I don't see why not. We're on holidays after all."

"What's a string qu-a-a?" Kit's voice fell silent, the new word defeating him.

"It's a group of four people, poppet, who play stringed instruments. Have you ever seen a violin?"

"I think I have." Kit eyed her doubtfully.

Katey gave an explosive little giggle. "Yes, you have. Great-aunt Zoe plays the violin. You know she holds it up like this." Katey went through elaborate sawing motions.

"Oh!" Kit laughed, just barely remembering.

"I'll show you a picture, Kit." Christy stroked his check. "The string section is the very heart of an orchestra. An orchestra is lots of people playing together using different instruments. Other people go along to hear them, to enjoy the music they make."

"We have a very good orchestra at our school," Katey told her with considerable pride. "At your school, too, Kit. Daddy's old school when you're ready to go."

"I'm never going to school." Kit's adorable face was troubled by a frown. "I'm staying home with Mummy."

Christy smoothed his glossy curls. "Don't worry about that now, Kit. We're going to have fun today. It might be good if we learn something about the instruments that go into an orchestra. We could find pictures of them. Trumpets, trombones, tubby the tuba, the drums that go bang and the cymbals that go clang. Then there's the violin and its big sister the viola, the bigger cello and the huge double bass. I'm sure there's a book in the library we could find. Uncle Ashe would be so pleased if you knew something about the instruments the musicians will play Saturday night."

"Is there going to be a big barbecue?" Kit asked in a hopeful voice.

It's one way to feed a lot of people informally, Christy mused. "Everyone on the station is invited. People from neighbouring stations, too. Today we're going to decide where we're all going to eat, then where we're all going to sit to listen to the music."

"Aren't we going to the Great Hall?" Katey questioned. "It's really *big*. Bigger than our great hall at school."

"I thought a concert under the stars would be lovely, Katey." Christy turned to the children for approval. "What do you think?"

Both children were silent for a moment then they looked up at her, sapphire eyes identically set shining.

"And I can cook the sausages." Kit grinned.

"You can't. You're too little," Katey scolded. "But I can pass some to you to eat." Sweetly she took her little brother's hand. "Come on. Let's get dressed."

"Let's." Kit began to jump up and down with excitement. "We really like you, Christy," he cried.

"Ditto, little pal." She put out a hand and they all slapped a high five.

It took only a few days for Christy and the children to settle into a routine that still allowed Christy time to herself. As Ashe had told her at the beginning, Lonnie had staff to help her keep such a very big house in order, aboriginal girls who had been born on the station, went away for schooling after age eight, the cut-off point for the small station school, then chose to return to their families and their desert home, the land of their ancestors and totemic spirits. This was the place where they were happiest. The homeland. One of the girls, Metta, was particularly good with the children, gentle but firm, and it was to her Christy turned most often for help. What was perfect about Metta, Christy considered, was she had remarkable artistic skill, which Christy was soon to discover was inherent in Metta's ancient race.

Metta knew exactly how to keep the children entertained; teaching them how to model good likenesses of desert animals with the Play-Doh Christy had had the foresight to bring with her, teaching them quick methods to get started with the drawing and painting, stimulating them with ideas and stories from the Dreamtime. The results were surprisingly pleasing. Both children, perhaps because they *were* little children, showed an artistic bent, painting on the small square boards Metta provided; part of a hoard Metta's little brothers and sisters kept for their paintings. An area in Christy's sitting room was fast getting covered with examples of the childrens' painting skills, which they intended to take home to show their parents.

Christy was well aware aboriginal art was finding an increasingly wide market both at home and overseas, particularly the U.S.A. with many of the major artists' work being bought up by city galleries, and allotted a hefty price. It was the dealers who got far and away the largest cut, sometimes as high as fifty per cent. There scarcely seemed to be an aboriginal community, particularly in the central desert areas and the Northern Territory, that didn't have at least two highly gifted artists among them all committed to passing on their "stories" and technical skills to their children.

Christy who had always been attracted to aboriginal paintings felt enormously pleased when Metta suggested she might like to visit one of the camps of the desert nomads who frequently stayed on Augusta for varying periods in between walkabouts. The relationship between the McKinnons and the indigenous people had developed over a century or more into a happy arrangement, almost a "family" arrangement where the aboriginal people led a healthy, protected life with employment for all. Aborigines made fine stockmen, fencers, mechanics. Their wives and daughters worked on various jobs around the station, saddle makers, boot makers, basket weavers, whip makers, or on domestic duties up at the homestead. The aboriginal children attended the small station school along with the children of the white and part-white employees. Ashe McKinnon, as young as he was, was regarded as a father figure, a good man, a kind man, the provider.

Riding lessons, much to the children's excited delight, were started on. The basics at least, getting each child to feel comfortable and happy aloft. Neither child had even so much as sat on a horse, so Christy was surprised at the ease and fearlessness they displayed when first lifted into the saddle. Indeed four-year-old Kit sat even more securely than his older sister with a natural balance.

Ashe had provided, from a splendid stable that quite fired Christy's imagination, a beautiful little white pony, Milk Opal. As expected, Opal was sweet-tempered and well-schooled, so the first "lessons" proved a very enjoyable experience with Christy walking around a gravelled enclosure adjacent to the large and fascinating stables complex which employed a lot of historic materials in the construction, holding a leading rein. It was a fortunate start for both children, because not only was Christy an accomplished horsewoman, she had the ability to gain the childrens' attention and impart the basics in such a way they couldn't wait for the next riding lesson.

For her own enjoyment Ashe had provided her with a beautiful mount, Desert Dancer, a supple, balanced animal eager and responsive to her every command. So it evolved Christy started the day with her own early morning ride managing to be back at the homestead just as the children were getting under way. With all the activity and fresh air the children had no problems getting off to sleep, generally going right through until around half past seven when Christy returned.

Christy had already told Ashe what she planned for the concert. He listened, gave her carte blanche to do as she pleased, along with two of the station's carpenters to build a rotunda on the homestead grounds. One of those delightful little timber gazebos that fit perfectly into the desert environment. It was here Christy was hoping the musicians would play. Lighting could be arranged. To be easily accessible to everyone, the concert would be viewed and heard in the round.

The children predictably thought it was marvellous, checking on proceedings each day. "I'm going to adore it," Katey cried, lying on the grass and looking up through the silver-green leaves of a gum to the blue chinks of sky. "Will we be able to play in it after?"

"Of course. We could bring our lunch out here." Really there were so many things to do, so many areas of the great station to see Christy thought it would take a lifetime to acquaint herself with Augusta.

She and Lonnie conferred for enjoyable hours on the food they would serve. Nothing elaborate but a little bit different from the usual barbecue, though food became almost irrestible when cooked over flames in the outdoors. Fifty people including eight young children had to be fed and she'd decided a barbecue was the perfect way to do it. Permanent brick barbecues, massive to Christy's eyes, had long since been constructed in sheltered areas a little way from the rear of the house and the pool area, but with easy access to the kitchen.

In the end it was planned on the classic peppered Augusta beef steaks in beer and garlic; barbecued lamb with a lavender balsamic marinade; sweet-and-sour kebabs, both lamb and chicken, and the obligatory char-grilled beef burgers for the children, all served with cool, crisp garden salads, the perfect foil to barbecued food, plus a sweet-and-sour onion salad and a spiced aubergine salad which, Lonnie told Christy, Mr. Ashe and the men particularly liked. Potato wedges tossed in fragrant garlicky olive oil with fresh chopped rosemary were decided on to add the extra dimension. For a while they considered flying in fresh barramundi, the great eating fish of the tropics, from North Queensland or the Territory, but decided they really had enough. Dessert would be barbecued fruits served with whipped cream, ice cream, a chocolate fondue or all three. The people who would help with the cooking, men and women, were all judged excellent both at operating the barbecues and cooking the food.

"You don't need to do anything, darlin', you know," Lonnie told Christy in her kindly fashion, "not on the night. You'll want to enjoy yourself."

"I'll be enjoying myself helping," Christy insisted.

''Well we'll have to make an early start,'' Lonnie grinned. ''Even a barbecue takes a lot of work. But you're a great organizer. Mr. Ashe agrees.''

By four-thirty late Saturday afternoon, the musicians and guests from neighbouring stations had arrived and been installed either in guest bedrooms at the homestead or, in the case of single men, in one of the stockmen's dormitories where they would get at most a few hours' sleep. Entertainments in the isolated Outback aren't all that frequent, consequently the most was made of any that came along.

Everyone appeared in high good humour, though Christy was sometimes uncomfortably aware there was considerable speculation as to her presence on Augusta and her exact position in Ashe McKinnon's life. This was a man as eligible as they came. They remembered the girlfriends he had over the years. Two stood out.

One was Gemma Millner-Hill who had come along with her parents and two of her unmarried brothers to enjoy the entertainment. Christy had no difficulty in recognising Gemma. She was the best-looking of Callista's bridesmaids. The one who had grabbed Ashe's arm at the reception, demanding to know why he had been so cruel to her.

Gemma, for her part, was so shocked when she first laid eyes on Christy, she couldn't hide it, her fine, faintly sharp features drawing together so tightly it gave her a pinched look. This was the girl who had captivated so many at Callista's wedding. The mystery woman no one knew a thing about except Ashe, the hardest man in the world to pin down, who had stayed glued to her side all night. Anger, concern, jealousy and bitterness welled in Gemma's heart.

All these emotions were registered by Christy as Gemma grimly regarded her. One didn't have to be a mind reader to realise Gemma had an enormous attachment to Ashe, an attachment that was shared by her parents and two tall, lean, attractive brothers who nevertheless couldn't tear their eyes away from Christy even as they were greeting Ashe with great enthusiasm and pumping his hand.

''So, who's the beautiful lady?'' Dalton, the elder, demanded to know, staring with an expectant, eager face at Christy.

Ashe turned to where Christy was standing, putting out an arm. "Christy, you don't know the Millner-Hill family, do you?"

Christy smiled and stepped forward dutifully, refusing to be upset by the veiled hostility that emanated from the Millner-Hill women, even as they kept their feelings at bay with big social smiles.

"I do remember Gemma from Callista's wedding but I don't think we actually met," Christy said pleasantly.

"I don't think anyone missed *you.*" Gemma's smile just missed out on being a sneer. "Aside from your blond hair and your beauty we all wondered who you were. I mean we all thought we knew Ashe's friends."

"Apparently not *all* of them," Ashe intervened smoothly, beginning the introductions through which Gemma was sufficiently off balance as to glower. Not so the men of the family, who responded with considerable warmth. Mrs. Millner-Hill could barely keep the dismay out of her eyes as she queried, "You're staying here, dear?" She stared very hard at Christy with her piercingly blue eyes.

"Looking after the children really," Christy supplied casually when she felt under threat.

"Ashe's cousin, Nicole, and her husband are having a holiday."

"Of course we *know* Nicole and Brendan," Gemma informed her just a bit too shortly. "Nic and I have shared a special friendship for many years now. So you're something of a nursemaid? You get paid for it?"

Again Ashe bestirred his tall elegant body, saying suavely, "Christine is my *guest,* Gemma. I'm the one who put pressure on her to come out here. Nic definitely needed a break so Christy offered to mind the children. They're taking a nap so they can be awake for the concert, or at least part of it. They don't want to miss out. You'll see them later," he promised.

"That would be lovely!" Mrs. Millner-Hill gushed at the same time, making it sound like she was heaving a great sigh. Ashe and Gemma may have broken up a year back but Mrs. Millner-Hill had never given up hope they would be reunited. Ashe, marvellous as he was, was such a difficult man. He set up his own games; playing by his own rules. A very difficult man to catch. Now this blond girl who looked as intelligent as she was beautiful was staying in the homestead. Unchaperoned.

It was intensely upsetting. Mrs. Millner-Hill could only guess at how poor darling Gemma was feeling.

In fact Gemma's emotional turbulence was threatening to get out of hand. Jealousy bubbled inside her like a witch's cauldron. As far as she was concerned, her relationship with Ashe had only been interrupted. Something would bring them together again. She'd lived on hope. If it took her all night she'd find out where Christy Parker came from and exactly who she was. One thing was certain, she wasn't on home turf.

The food was served early as a concession to the children in the audience. Christy and her helpers had set out tables and chairs in the rear garden, the tables covered with chequered patio cloths with bright napkins. A whole range of colourful plates had been chosen, as well, with a little candle-lit lantern centre table. White fairy lights decorated nearby trees, lights streamed from the house and round the pool, the turquoise surface floating masses of wild hibiscus and candles. It looked very pretty even if someone would have a job clearing the pool the next day.

Around seven o'clock they all came together at the front of the homestead for the concert, settling themselves on the lawn on chairs from the piled stack, or on rugs and blankets, the children sprawling out full-length with their chins propped up beneath their hands.

Christy glanced around at the happy expectant faces, disconcerted to catch sight of Ashe and Gemma standing beneath a sparkling lit gum in intense conversation. Or it certainly looked that way.

For a moment Christy was overcome by a sense of not belonging. All these people knew one another. Their families had been neighbours for generations. It was only to be expected their loyalties would be with one of their own. Although Ashe had never spoken about Gemma, it was obvious at one time they'd had a shared personal relationship. Something was driving Gemma to behave with the jealousy that was so badly apparent. The momentum had led her to cornering Ashe. Christy glanced away quickly as though she were a voyeur, pushing a cushion beneath dear little Kit to make him more comfortable.

It was time to start.

The music was beautiful. Dvorak, Tchaikovsky, Borodin. It was wonderfully melodious, at times so meltingly lovely it brought tears to Christy's eyes. Each member of the quartet was a fine musician in their own right yet they presented a most satisfying impression of ''oneness,'' of ''wholeness,'' that was deeply touching and deeply spiritual. There was no intermission to break the spell. Indeed everyone in the rapt audience wanted the spell to continue. Afterwards such was the collective experience there was complete silence for a few moments broken by the call of a night bird, before every man, woman and child broke into long, loud applause.

They were favoured with two encores from the group then one of the violinists broke into excerpts from Gershwin's *Porgy and Bess,* starting with ''Summertime,'' which everyone knew and greeted with delight.

Christy had shared her rug with the children; now it was time for them to go to bed.

''Can't we stay, Christy?'' Katey begged.

''Impossible, darling, you're drowsy as it is. Your eyes are half closing and just look at Kit! It was wonderful though, wasn't it?''

"I'm going to ask Daddy if I can learn the violin as soon as I get home," Katey vowed. "I knew some of those pretty songs."

"Let me guess." Christy smiled down at the child. "I think it would be Borodin, the Russian composer. The melodies were turned into songs for a movie called *Kismet*."

Katey, by this time, was freely yawning. "Here's Uncle Ashe," she cried. Christy turned around. She had no idea where he had sat.

"Time for bed, you two?" He joined them, going down on his haunches. "Enjoy it?" He tickled Kit.

"It was good," Kit said, still hearing the music in his head. While Katey threw her arms around Ashe's neck and kissed him.

"What about if I carry you, Kit?" Ashe suggested, seeing the little boy was all but asleep.

"On your back," Kit begged.

Ashe stayed until the children were tucked up in bed, their eyelids dropping the minute their heads touched the pillows.

He followed Christy out into the hallway. "That went very well. The programme was just right. Beautiful melodies, some of them quite familiar, everyone could enjoy."

"*I* loved it," Christy said, a little in conflict—pain and delight.

"I think everyone else did, too." He took hold of her by the shoulders and brought her back against the wall.

"So what next?" She looked up at him cautiously. What did she really know about this man, only that he was the most glamorous, exciting creature, from another vastly different world?

"Well first of all I'd like to thank you for getting it all together," he murmured, staring down at her. The wall sconce gleamed on her hair and the purity of her skin.

"I had help," she said shakily, as his magnetism took over.

"Nevertheless you brought it off with panache. The settings, the food. A woman can make things so much more elegant."

"Well thank you." Colour warmed her eyes and her cheeks. "But you could have asked Gemma." She hadn't intended to say that, it just burst from her.

"I asked *you*." He lifted a thick strand of her hair, as he had often done before, curled it around his wrist then let it drop.

"Were you ever in love with her?"

"I told you before, Christy," he said softly. "I find it hard to describe love."

"Put it another way. Did you sleep with her?"

He took her face between his hands. "What business is it of yours? Surely my masculinity will suffer if I say I've never slept with a woman."

"I take it the answer is yes." She went a little limp.

"Why should it worry you?" he asked gently, reading her expression.

"Because I'm not stupid."

"You mean you think I may be working my way up to you?"

She was startled, defensive. "You *have* made a beginning."

"But then, Christy, I thought you were enjoying it?"

"Up to a point." She hardly knew what she was saying the excitement was so extreme.

"Then let's get married." He suggested it as calmly as he might have said, Let's camp out under the stars.

"What?" Her voice was so brittle it cracked.

''I said let's get married,'' he repeated patiently. ''You want commitment. I'm fighting the never-ending urge to take you to my bed. If you like we can announce our engagement.''

She backed right against the wall. ''So later on we can have a test run?'' Her green eyes were scathing, her body quivering with nerves.

''That's not what I asked you. I'm tired of waiting for cupid's arrow to hit me, aren't you?''

She watched his face, his mouth, those brilliant mocking eyes.

''How do you know cupid's arrow *hasn't* hit me?'' she retaliated, feeling slightly unbalanced.

''Deakin doesn't count.'' His voice had sting. ''You're not in love with *me,* are you?''

''You don't think I'm fool enough to say yes?'' Too late she regained some control. She tried to push past him but he stopped her.

''There's a good side to this, Christy.'' He brought up one arm, resting it against the wall beside her. ''I think we're suited. You're beautiful and clever. You feel safe and happy in my world. Don't worry, I've been observing you. You're gentle and kind, I see you with the children, with the staff. Lonnie already adores you. Metta is all Miss Christy says this, Miss Christy says that.... You have a delicate, sensitive hand.''

''I hope so,'' she said seriously. ''I believe in being myself. Anyway, both Lonnie and Metta have plenty to teach me. As for you? I think this is part of your plan to keep your ex-girlfriends away. Like Gemma for instance.''

His mouth twitched. ''I could have sworn Gemma had forgotten all about me.''

''But tonight she told you differently?''

''Why do you say that?'' he challenged, eyes narrowing.

''Because I happened to catch the two of you talking before the concert started.''

He gave a brief laugh. ''Christy, Christy, is there no privacy? Gemma is a great one for questions. I think we could stop all the talk in its tracks.''

''So there is talk?'' She knew it. She could feel it. Why not? Gossip was what most people did.

Ashe shrugged. ''You know how people are. Everyone has been waiting for me to get married from the day I turned eighteen. God knows why. I have to tell you, I have a horror of pushy mothers.''

''Especially when they look like Mrs. Millner-Hill?''

He shrugged good-humouredly. ''Little do you know the tricks Gwen has got up to in her time and she's taught Gemma everything she knows.''

''At least you didn't jilt her?'' Christy said, her expression turning melancholy.

''Please don't hark back to your little fling with Josh Deakin or I might really lose it.'' A flame in his dark eyes flickered. She looked luminescent, blooming like some extraordinarily beautiful flower.

The air was suddenly very still, heavy with a tension that ran just beneath their outpouring of words.

''Go on, lose it.'' Uncharacteristically she provoked him, defying the steely core in him. ''There's no one to see you.''

It was the match to the fuse. He pulled her forcefully into his arms, allowing her little room to manoeuvre, certainly no escape. His kiss was wild and swift. Passion burst like a damn. It was useless and dishonest to pretend she didn't want this, her body reacting with strange abandon as the tumult rolled over her.

He released her after a spinning eternity, looking for a moment like he wanted to slam his hand into the wall. "You're driving me crazy. You sure as hell know how."

Her long silky hair swept over her shoulder. "The world is full of sexy women," she taunted, desperate to pierce his emotional armour.

"Not like you. Not a chance."

"So how could we live happily ever after?" she questioned wildly. "I could be just like your mother. I have her hair."

His striking dark face was suddenly very still. "You've seen her portrait?"

"No I haven't." Her hostility collapsed like a pack of cards. "What are you doing, Ashe? What are *we* doing?"

"God knows." The admission was torn from him. "All I know is I want you to stay."

"You can't mean forever?" She knew now how empty her life would be without this complicated man in it.

His tension increased. With Christy he was experiencing something he had never experienced before. Tragedy had touched him deeply, for all his self-reliance, and it had left deep scars. He knew better than anybody ''love'' laid a man open to a kind of dying when that love was withdrawn. There was a price to be paid for everything. What he felt for this woman, right from the moment he'd set eyes on her, had made him vulnerable. In its way it had opened him up to suffering. He'd survived from childhood by developing an impregnable shell. Yet this beautiful creature was opening up a thousand cracks every day. He wanted her. God knows how he wanted her! He really *liked* her, everything about her. He felt nourished, as were the children, by her company. Was that love? Some very strong thread held them. She was as aware of it as he was. Yet he was rushing her headlong off her feet at a time when she too was vulnerable. He couldn't stop...couldn't... The knowledge he was a driven man mocked him. He could see the little diamond pricks of emotion in her eyes, large and glistening.

''You must be missing what I'm saying, Christy,'' he offered more quietly, not letting his ravaging emotions out. He took her fingertips and brought them to his mouth. ''I want you. Not for some tempestuous affair. I know it's been all too urgent. The timing! But I don't have a lot of time. You know that. I want you with a gold wedding band on your finger. If I were honest I'd admit I want to lock you up so you can't escape me.''

She saw stars. Then her vision cleared. ''You're manoeuvring me, Ashe.'' She knew full well a rational argument, even a play for her own integrity, wouldn't stand up against the feelings he aroused in her. ''I don't even know if I want to escape you but I'm frightened of getting in so deep I can't find the shore. I'm only seeing thc tip of the iceberg with you. I don't think you realise what a force you are.''

Challenge spilled from his brilliant eyes. ''You're not afraid to cope with it. I'm not wicked. I'm not ruthless. Dogged maybe. Why don't we try easy stages? A trial engagement.'' Smoothly he slipped back to humour, a cover-up for his deeper feelings. ''It would have to be a big wedding, I'm afraid. It will be expected. And you will make an exquisite bride. Don't you think we could live together, Christy?''

His sexual radiance, which she was seeing more and more of, vanquished her. She dropped her gaze before he could spot the tears that sprang into her eyes. How could she deal with him?

"Christy?" Like the most perfect lover he drew her into his arms with boundless tenderness, lowering his dark head to brush his cheek against the silk of her hair. "Don't cry. Please don't cry. Your tears bother me terribly."

Such an infinity of emotion!

Christy tried to get her thoughts together so she could deal with what was happening to her but this man made her perfectly good brain mush. "What you're trying to do, Ashe, is marry me off," she said in a subdued voice. "You're putting a lot of effort into it. The only odd part is you're trying to marry me off to *you*. You don't love me. Love to you is the forbidden word."

He was immersed in her intoxicating fragrance yet he held her back from him, and gave her *that* smile.

"I haven't heard you saying you love me," he countered, staring down at her.

It was her moment to tell him she had fallen head over heels in love with him, but she had her own needs. Self-protection. She would have to guard her heart. Retain her own identity.

"Christy. It's not like you to be tongue-tied."

In among the swirling emotions she was conscious of her frightened heart. "I'm scared you don't trust me, Ashe. You plucked me out of my life. You brought me here. Maybe at one level you're trying to keep me out of the way."

"Out of the reach of Deakin?" He sounded stern.

"Half a continent away," she continued, determined to have this out. "I don't love him, Ashe. I never did. I can see that very clearly now."

"I just hope you keep seeing it," he said bluntly.

At the fierceness in his black eyes rebellion swept up from the depths of her being. "What did I just say about trust?" she accused him, pulling away. The normal charm of her expression turned tempestuous. "No man and woman can have a good relationship without that."

"What we have is enough!" He knew he could ruin everything but was too caught up in the strength and urgency of ferocious emotion. He thought he could see her heart beating. Her breasts—he longed to caress them—rose and fell, stirring the white silk top that she wore. It was beautiful, stylish, sewn with pink flowers like the paper daisies that covered Augusta after rain. He could smell her delicate fragrance in his nostrils. She was herself. Who was he? A man who needed shock treatment to reveal his heart.

"There's something wrong with your thinking, Ashe," she told him sadly, unknowingly confirming his own thoughts. Christy was acutely aware of the conflict going on in him. It was going on in her. It was impossible for either of them to be calm. Why didn't she tell him what she wanted from him was *everything!* Not the unfathomable unknown.

Seeing her unrest, Ashe curbed his own upheaval, trying to shift some weight of grief off his heart. "Sexual attraction is a powerful thing, Christy. But what we have doesn't stop at that. If you marry me you can have it all. My horse, my kingdom…" His vibrant voice, so recently harsh, turned to mock-begging. "What I need is what every man needs. A good woman. I'd cross the desert on foot to reach her. But she's right here. You'll do just fine."

How could she possibly answer that? His voice held such endless promise, thrilling excitement. When he bent his head to kiss her, Christy surrendered completely to the torrent of desire that engulfed her.

An unstoppable force had entered her life. Now the force was sweeping her away.

CHAPTER SIX

GEMMA, on the pretext of wanting to see more of "darling Nic's children," begged for an extra day or so.

"If that's okay with you, Ashe," she cajoled, her warm friendly smile covering a shocking resentment. In fact resentment was too tame a word. Gemma was furious at Christy's presence in the house. Nevertheless she added, "Besides, I'll be company for Christy."

Christy almost winced. That was good. As good as it gets. Gemma's stay-over had more to do with being with Ashe than it had to do with her or the children. When Ashe gave his assent—what else could the man do short of scowling darkly and saying no—Gemma's mood lifted to something approaching buoyant.

The truth was, Gemma had made a career out of waiting for Ashe to ask her to marry him. After all, he hadn't asked anyone else. There were at least a dozen with ambitions, but no one quite as desperate as Gemma to get him for a husband. There was nothing wrong with her, certainly. It might have been straining it a bit to say she was beautiful, but she was good-looking, competent, intelligent, healthy. She was station born and bred; her family was highly respected within the pastoral industry. She knew Ashe had a deep-seated wariness of city women. Of course it all had to do with the trauma of his mother running off. According to Gemma's own mother, Eve McKinnon might have been very beautiful with fascinating thrown in, but she was absolutely hopeless as a station wife. No good at all. Not a *real* station wife.

Many were the stories Gwen Millner-Hill told about "the bolter," which was how she always referred to Ashe's runaway mother. Sometimes Gemma thought deep down her mother actually had hated the beautiful Eve. But then she had so admired Ashe's father. Everyone's sympathies had been with McKinnon and the young Ashe. Which made it all the more astonishing Ashe had a city girl with a mane of liquid gold in his house.

It didn't make sense—any of it—but then Ashe had always been unknowable, constantly confusing her just when she thought she knew him. After a hurried discussion—both saw it as an emergency—Gemma had sent her mother home to run a check on Christine Parker. They should have done it before now but neither of them had had the least idea Ashe had invited the young woman to the station.

Nicole hadn't even called her, Gemma thought, feeling outrage and betrayal. At least Nic could have done that. She desperately needed the warning. She would have gladly kept an eye on the children if it were only for a short time. Children could be very demanding, even tiresome, but the housekeeper was there on call. It would have been wonderful to live in the same house as Ashe, Gemma thought, her anger and disappointment building up to grief. It would have given her so many opportunities to get closer to him. It would have been like old times when they were friends. Real friends, laughing and talking together.

How had this Christy Parker found her way into his life? Gemma, with the help of her mother, was determined to find out. They had a few clues. None of their friends had seen her at the actual wedding ceremony. No way they could have missed her. She was too eye-catching. It made Gemma want to scream. For that matter didn't Ashe have a down on blondes? How then did this particular blonde manage to get into the reception? She had to be a guest from the bridegroom's side. Josh Deakin, legal eagle. At least they had a fix on him....

Although it was still early morning, silvery-blue heat waves danced across the vast open plains. It was an unending landscape, extending to the horizon with the golden spinifex decorating the wind-sculpted sands and the rippling slopes. As the wind shifted so did the fascinating sand patterns that the aborigines depicted so often in their paintings. The dormant seeds of the flowering annuals and ephemerals that came to blazing life after the rains lay quietly beneath the fiery earth as a child lies quietly beneath a blanket. Christy had heard many times of the great glory of the desert heart when it burst into blossom, now she wondered if she would ever see it.

The Wet Season in the tropical north was almost due, bringing monsoonal rainfall to the great desert region via the interlocking river system but very rarely to the Red Centre. Could she be so lucky? There were many photographs on her sitting room wall of McKinnon family members and friends standing amid the floral splendour of Augusta after rain. From sandhill desert to the greatest garden on earth.

Christy sat the beautiful chestnut, Desert Dancer, looking out over the shimmering landscape. This was a favourite vantage point atop one of the low eroded escarpments that dotted the station; the sandstone layered in pink, white, red and yellow. The cattle looked small from this distance. A section of the great herd was grazing the desert floor, finding nourishment and moisture in the pink parakeelya, a flowering succulent peculiar to the sandhills. Stock could live for months on the parakeelya without the need for water. So even in the desert nature provided. Indeed the Great Artesian Basin lay beneath the Simpson Desert. There were springs and waterholes around the desert borders, but no permanent water in the desert proper. Christy had been told the aborigines looked on the desert proper as a place inhabited by evil spirits. So far she could only see its phenomenal primeval beauty.

She marvelled at the splendour of the waterlilies that crowded every waterhole on the station; pink, blue, white, each billabong turning on a display of the one colour. She hadn't so far seen a mix. But then Augusta was so vast she didn't think she could take it all in even if she had a lifetime to do it. She had, however, experienced a marvellous ''connection'' that had to do with her love of nature in all its moods. Or perhaps the desert only sang its songs to certain people. She could well appreciate how many people would be daunted by this wild environment. The station was so remote; women in particular could be frightened of its loneliness, emptiness, and its ''other world'' antiquity. Perhaps that was what had happened to Ashe's mother? She may well have tried but been overcome by a lifestyle so extreme, so polarized from the one she'd been used to. There was no use asking Ashe. He didn't want to talk.

Christy looked about the desert heartland amazed by the fiery clash of colours as the sun rose higher. The tops of the desert oaks looked to be on fire. Ashe had warned her to keep a sharp eye out for wild camels, dingoes on the prowl and the herds of wild donkeys that roamed the station, but so far she had only witnessed the thrilling sight of herds of kangaroos, both the desert euros and the more nomadic Red bounding their way across the heavy red sand or the sandstone bluffs of the hill country. Ashe had promised to take her to the caves, which held fine examples of aboriginal drawings. She was looking forward to that but she realised Ashe had little spare time especially in the lead up to the annual big muster.

Descending the rocky slope with its flying pebbles glittering like glass in the sun, Christy kept her eye out for the brightly patterned bearded and netted dragons, the lizards that were widely distributed all over the area. Although they looked extraordinary, even fearsome, they were harmless. Dancer was well behaved but she didn't want her mount startled. This was the home, too, of the biggest lizard of them all, the goanna. She wasn't so keen on being confronted by one of them. Many more than six feet long, they could, and often did, present a problem. In addition to the desert's beauty there were always the hazards, but mercifully most desert animals kept out of man's way.

Christy loved these early morning rides. The desert showed a softer mood with long shadows falling over the dunes, delineating each ripple, revealing the tracks of the mulga scrub spiders, the marsupials, the reptiles and all the other night hunters. She could explore this place forever, but the children were always on her mind.

Safely on the plain, Christy let Dancer have her head. The chestnut thoroughbred was a wonderful ride, highly intelligent and hardy, with no reduction in speed and mobility over the sand. Christy was getting to know more about the station's breeding programme of the Australian stock horse with its strong infusion of thoroughbred blood. Desert Dancer was not a workhorse but a thoroughbred kept for the single great pleasure of riding.

Nearing the home complex Christy eased Dancer up. Lonnie had told her she could always take her time, but Lonnie had quite enough to do, especially after the weekend, which had proved such a great success. Usually, Christy looked forward to getting back to the homestead, to sitting down to breakfast with the children, but not today.

Gemma was still in residence even after two full days of her self-invited stay.

Gemma, to Christy's surprise after confiding her desire to get to know the children better, showed no real interest in them. A state of affairs that wasn't missed by the perceptive children. She had also proved arrogant and unsympathetic in her dealing with Metta, going so far as to challenge Christy's decision to allow the children so much time in Metta's company. On a sad note, Christy concluded Gemma was one of those people who didn't believe in encouraging any sort of friendship with the indigenous people, though she would have been highly affronted had anyone labelled her a "racist." One way and another Gemma had thrown quite a few discordant notes into what had been a harmonious holiday.

Children were excellent judges of adult behaviour. Gemma hadn't fooled them. Christy thought of last night's pre-bed conversation with wry humour... ''Do you think she'll go tomorrow?'' Katey had asked, blue eyes anxious.

''I really couldn't say, poppet.'' Christy shrank away from saying anything unkind about Gemma much as she deserved it.

"Why does she keep saying, 'if you want my opinion'?" Katey mimicked Gemma's lofty tones comically.

"Oh well, it's an expression..."

"She doesn't like you, Christy," Katey, six going on sixty, told her owlishly. "She never ever says anything nice to you but she definitely likes Uncle Ashe. I 'spose she wants to marry him."

"Gosh I hope she doesn't," Kit suddenly sat up to yell. "I don't like her."

"Neither do I." Katey nodded her head emphatically. "We had such fun when she wasn't around. I'm going to say a prayer her father comes in his plane to pick her up."

Amen to that, had been Christy's silent contribution as she turned off the light.

There was definitely a downside to having Gemma around.

Less than half a mile away, riding back to the homestead, Ashe was thinking much the same thing. He had really stretched himself trying to find time to take Christy and the children on a tour of the station but he didn't fancy taking Gemma along. In fact the very thought was making him so irritable he was close to grinding his teeth. It sure was a difficult thing to put a woman like Gemma off. Harder yet when she had a mother like Gwen.

The worst thing he had ever done was partner Gemma a few times at various Outback functions. Once a post-polo ball. What the hell! He had known her all his life. He had kissed her. God knows she had expected it. He had never slept with her. He hadn't been fool enough to complicate their lives, yet a few kisses had somehow given Gemma and her mother the idea suitability and availability was a big factor in arranging a marriage. Something like his own fool argument. Even Gemma's father and brothers had cottoned onto the idea.

He didn't know why he was being so polite, except Gemma was a guest and he liked to keep a rein on a tongue that tended to be sardonic to the point of cutting. But Gemma's jealousy of Christy was becoming very tedious. Surely, Gemma was supposed to be getting to know the children better when so far as he could see she hadn't bothered with them at all. Also because he knew her so well he was convinced Gemma had something up her sleeve. Some little bombshell she was awaiting just the right moment to explode.

Ashe sent his horse plunging down a steep sandy slope, taking a short cut so he could meet up with Christy after her morning ride. Gemma had hardly let Christy get a word in at the dinner table last night. In fact she was acting pretty much like she was the future mistress of Augusta station and Christy a tolerated guest. Christy was really being very nice about the whole thing but he doubted very much if he could put up with much more.

From a distance off Christy could see Ashe coming at a strong pacc towards her, red dust rising like smoke from his horse's hooves. Immediately her heart started its mad fluttering and, unknown to her, her whole face became illuminated with pleasure and excitement. It was very difficult to get a handle on all her soaring emotions when she was so overwhelmed by everything, the station, its environment, the spiritual effects of the ancient desert, and above all, her feelings for Ashe McKinnon. They were so powerful they had invaded every aspect of her life.

After Josh's treachery, which she now saw as a godsend, she had expected to go through a serious emotional slump. Instead in meeting Ashe she felt something momentous had occurred. She had fallen madly in love with him. Rebound? *Irrational love?* That's what Ashe would call it. ''Hormones.'' Except she admired and respected him. Everyone on the station did. There had never been any doubt Ashe could carry on from his father; carry on the proud tradition of the McKinnon cattle kings. And this man had asked her to marry him! Why hadn't she said yes there and then? Marriage to Ashe would be a tremendous experience.

Surely she could face the task of getting him to love her, to look on her as the most important woman in his life. She recognised the fact the sad destruction of his parents' marriage, brought about by his mother's adultery—one had to face it—and her subsequent pregnancy had resulted in Ashe's acute cynicism about marriage and women. Given it was a terrible story, including as it did his own abandonment at such a young age, why couldn't she change all that? The very thought made her dizzy.

Whether it was with exhilaration or trepidation she wasn't quite sure.

He was beautiful to look at, riding a handsome white stallion with classic ease and grace. She knew that bred in the saddle he could tackle anything. Station life itself was dangerous. Musters alone were savagely demanding on horse and rider, the wild environment full of challenges. Stockmen had to develop unique handling skills and the stamina for travelling great distances. She knew from her own experiences one had to be fatalistic if one ''rode'' seriously. Ashe's splendid horsemanship showed.

''You really are a wonderful rider,'' she told him when he reined in alongside her, vivid, compelling, another colourful bandanna, this one yellow, tied loosely around his darkly tanned throat. ''A pleasure to watch.''

''Why thank you, ma'am.'' He swept his cream akubra off in response, giving her *that* smile, albeit mocking. ''I was hoping to meet up with you. In fact I made it my business.''

''Are you coming back to the house?'' She was acutely aware of his brilliant dark eyes moving over her, noting the way she wore her hair in a thick rope down her back.

''I had intended to, but sadly Gemma is getting on my nerves.''

''You did invite her,'' she couldn't resist pointing out.

His answer was a groan. ''I hate to say it but Gem invited herself. I'm just wondering when she intends to go?''

''Then you'd better ask before she decides to move in.''

You're the one I want to move in, he thought with such certainty the jolt radiated out from his heart. ''What do you suggest I say? Your jealousy of Christy is making me angry?''

''Is it?'' Christy challenged, staring into his eyes. ''Doesn't she mean *anything* to you?''

''She's a friend, what else?'' He shrugged impatiently. ''I've known her all her life.''

''Then why is she working so hard to convince me you shared a deep meaningful relationship?''

''Maybe to make trouble. Anyway it was never as deep and committed as your relationship with Deakin,'' he retorted very crisply.

''Give me a break!'' Christy sighed. ''I told you, Josh is ancient history.''

''Frankly I'm relieved to hear that.'' Ashe lifted his head to look up at a hovering falcon in search of prey. ''Because I've had word Josh and Callista want an invitation to Augusta. They've had to come home earlier than anticipated. Poor old Josh caught a tummy bug.'' Ashe didn't try hard to sound sincere. ''Apparently he did too much swooping on the wrong things to eat.''

''How unfortunate.'' Christy was more sincere in her comment. ''You've heard from them?''

''You mean *you* wish you had?'' he enquired acidly. ''I've heard from Mercedes.''

''And they want to come here?'' Christy levelled him with a dubious green stare.

''They want to meet up with Nic and Brendan when they pick up their children.''

''Good grief!'' Christy was stunned. A little distance away the falcon dropped like a stone to pick up a small rodent.

''Would you believe it?'' Ashe said with an exaggerated drawl. ''I hardly ever see them. Except at Christmas. Now *everyone* wants to come.''

''Then I'd better be making plans to go home.''

"Surely you want to see Josh again?" His handsome face wore its most infuriating expression. "Just to check on your feelings?"

"What I really want to do is smack that look off your face," Christy retorted with such spirit Dancer did a lively two-step.

"You want to go easy on the violence," he scoffed. "I just could retaliate."

"You'd never strike a woman." Christy looked and sounded aghast.

"Who said anything about striking? I was thinking something more lascivious. Anyway, as you know, I'm a man who likes to make his plans in advance. Forewarned is fore-armed."

"Meaning?" Christy had to pull a little on the reins. Dancer was getting restive.

"Why don't we find some shade?" Ashe suggested, cramming his akubra further down over his eyes. "I know you're looking after your beautiful skin but you really don't need too much sun. Let's make for the lagoon."

Why not? The lagoon was beautiful. "Why don't we have some fun while we're at it? Let's race."

Very provocatively he glanced down at his glinting watch. ''I'll give you a three-minute start.''

''Do you want to race or not?'' Such a rhythm was building up in her blood, the sensitive chestnut was responding.

''You're on,'' Ashe purred, leaning across the neck of his white stallion.

Christy took off like a rocket, never once looking back. She knew Ashe on that beautiful horse could overtake her and Dancer but she was going to give it her best shot. She could make the obvious diagonal cut across the open plain or...spreading out in front of them was a stretch of boulders which she had ridden around on at least two occasions...she could go over the top. She'd soared over fences and ditches many times before in her life. Jumping the boulder in the middle, the highest, would give her a distinct advantage.

What Christy hadn't calculated on as Desert Dancer stretched out in preparation to storm the barricade was that a rock wallaby, in the way of wallabies, chose that very moment to announce its presence, standing up on its hind legs and looking stupid. In a real test of horsemanship Christy held on, as rider and noble animal bccame airborne, landing cleanly on the other side but so explosively Christy, despite her best efforts, was thrown out of the saddle, the thick fleshy leaves on a spread of para-keelya and button grass absorbing much of the shock.

"My God!" Ashe's reaction initially frantic quickly turned to a curious anger when he found her lying flat out on the carpet of crushed succulents, spitting out bits of grass. "What the hell was that all about?" he de-manded, a mixture of high relief and perverse anger tearing at him.

She couldn't answer for a moment, waiting for her lungs to fill.

"Christy?" He dropped to his knees beside her. "You're okay, aren't you?"

She grasped his anger and tried to make light of things. "I would have been if that damned wallaby hadn't messed with us. How is Dancer?" She turned her head in concern.

"He's not hurt," Ashe assured her a little harshly. "He's as worried as I am that you didn't break a limb."

"I'm fine." She fixed her eyes at the blue sky not the burning urgency of his expression. "I'm a bit winded that's all. All this stuff—"

she clutched the pink flowers ''—broke my fall.''

''You're going to hurt someplace,'' he warned her.

''Without a doubt.''

''I hated watching that, you know,'' he burst out explosively as though it were a catastrophe.

''I can see that, Ashe.'' She lay quietly.

''You're supposed to take care of yourself.'' He frowned.

''Look, I'm not hurt.'' She could laugh still. ''I took a bit of a fall.''

''Try to sit up.'' He slid a hand beneath her back, his expression taut.

''Listen. I've fallen off plenty of horses over the years,'' she protested with a spark of defiance. ''I bet you have, too.''

''I don't want to see you do tricks.'' His voice cracked with authority. ''You're not a stunt rider.'' He stared down at her moodily, realising uncharacteristically he was unnerved. So it was his time to rediscover what caring meant. For a moment there, as she and the chestnut were airborne, he had known blind fear. Experience told him she was about to take a fall. It took very little to break one's neck.

Family tragedy had brought that starkly home to him. The defences he had painstakingly built up over the long years were about to be destroyed. Was this what he wanted? Loving a woman or living in limbo?

Christy, staring at his passionate, dynamic face was moved to say gently, "You're making too much of it, Ashe. I'm fine. It was Dancer I was most worried about."

"You owe it to me to take all possible care."

"I know. I'm sorry. It would have been perfectly all right only Dancer was spooked."

"Horses spook easily. You know that." He ran a checking hand along the length of her body, still frowning.

Christy knew she had to get to her feet; to prove to him nothing was broken, that she could move freely.

"There." Once up she gave him a smile, feeling she was drowning in love of him. "Ashe?"

He took her into his arms, trying to impose a hard control on his fraying nerves. "Promise me you won't attempt to do any jumping without wearing a hard hat, not that damned akubra," he ordered. "Make sure you know the terrain."

"Absolutely." She brought her face up, impervious to everything around her. Except him. Something had shifted in their largely invisible relationship. In front of the children and the staff Ashe treated her as "family," a younger cousin perhaps. Now he was coming out into the open. Maybe in throwing her, the filly had done her an enormous favour.

"I've got something for you," Ashe said, taking her hand and leading her toward the tree-lined lagoon.

"How very thoughtful of you. What is it?" She couldn't keep the excitement out of her voice, or her fingers from trembling in his.

He was regaining control now his voice resuming its habitual self-assurance. "I hope you like it but it shouldn't be a big surprise."

"Now you've got me very interested." Her head was aching a little so she dragged it out of its plait, shaking her hair free. "Isn't this a beautiful spot? Paradise before the fall. The waterlilies are exquisite. I never knew they existed in such great numbers or how sweetly they spike the air. I'm planning to come back even if I have to put up my tent." It was nothing more than a nervous outpouring but as she met his gaze the rest of her words caught in her throat. She wasn't at all sure what was about to happen except it was *significant;* life-changing.

Ashe took her left hand, first raising it to his mouth. His concentration on her was intense. Her hand still captured, he slid a glorious engagement ring down on her finger, cushioning the sudden spasm that passed through her body with his own.

"I offer you this ring, Christy, knowing that if you consent to wear it you will make me a proud man."

She felt her emotions were being pushed to extremity. She felt as though her heart would break. Tears pricked her eyes but she couldn't get out a word.

"It looks like I'll have to kiss you," Ashe murmured, brilliance in his expression. He bent his dark head, taking her mouth like he could draw her heart through her lips; kissing her until she was not only speechless but breathless. "Understand that I want you." He made no attempt to conceal his passionate emotion. "I need you. I need to have you for always."

Christy stared down tumultuously at their entwined hands; his so strong and lean, deeply tanned, hers, in comparison, milk-white. "This is something I could never have foreseen, Ashe," she told him, low-voiced. "We've known each other such a short time. It's like a great leap off a cliff."

"I'd leap off a cliff for you without a second thought." His beautiful black eyes were soft with a smile. "You can take as much time to think about it as you like. Maybe by tonight."

"Sorcerer!" She stared up at him, her green eyes huge.

"You haven't told me you like it." He lifted her hand, watching the flash of the exquisite precious stones.

"I've never seen a ring so startlingly lovely in my life."

"Like you. With *your* eyes it had to be an emerald." In fact a flawless Colombian square-cut emerald flanked by brilliant cut diamonds.

Christy honestly thought her legs would give way. Emotions, his and hers, stormed around them. He never said he loved her, even at that moment something was preventing him from forming the words, but everything else he did saturated her in a feeling she was loved. Loved as she had never been loved before. It was tantalising but deep and constant. She began to cry.

"Darling, Christy, please don't!" The words were ripped from him, the tender weight behind the endearment offering unlimited possibilities. "This is our new life." He bent down to softly kiss her open mouth, his tongue taking up her tears. "Don't be fearful. I won't ever let you down. This is a sacred promise. You have so much to give me. Everything I have is yours." It was way beyond the boundaries of any marriage contract, Christy thought ecstatically.

In fact Ashe's words, spoken in such a way, consumed her. Her heart was beating in rhapsodic time with the chirruping of the birds that flashed in and out of that enchanted place. "You trust me with your life?" To fail him was to be lost.

For an instant his striking face turned faintly bleak. "I trust the soul in you, Christy." He couldn't yet tell her of the loneliness and longings he had capped like a bottomless well.

His face swam before her eyes. She was flushed with high emotion. She could wait for him to tell her he loved her. A man with all that passion locked up in him had already paid too high a price for loving. "I'm going to do the very best I possibly can. I'm not dreaming this, am I?" Christy smiled through the dazzle of tears.

"No!" He drew her towards him like she was infinitely precious.

"Were you that sure of me you already had the ring?"

His laugh was deep in his throat. "I knew it would suit you from the moment I laid eyes on you. There are earrings to match. There was a necklace but somehow my mother got away with that. I might just try to get it back." A faint harshness crept into his tone. "Every piece belonged to my grandmother, my father's mother. My mother chose a ruby for her engagement ring. She didn't leave it behind. But she never wore your ring though she did wear the earrings with the necklace on grand occasions. If you prefer another ring or another stone you have only to say so. I want to tell you I loved my grandmother very much."

Tentatively Christy brought up her hand and touched his dark handsome face. "I love this ring, Ashe. It's so beautiful it takes my breath away.''

More than anything in the world she wanted his love. A vision of Ashe's mother as she imagined her sprang vividly into Christy's mind. Why did she have such doubts Ashe's mother had been utterly callous? Maybe leaving her small son had wrenched her heart out. No one seemed likely to ever know unless by some miracle Ashe was able to speak to his mother. Eve McKinnon's shocking and dramatic flight from Augusta had infected her son's soul. Now all Christy wanted was to make up for the lost years.

After such an experience Christy felt delirious for the rest of the day. Not even Gemma's abrasive presence could sap her of her joy though she couldn't find it in her heart to cause Gemma shock and upset by wearing her engagement ring. She and Ashe had decided they would announce their engagement officially when the family came home.

''The start of our marriage contract,'' Ashe had laughed without irony.

Christy knew Nicole and Brendan would be delighted. Possibly Callista would be greatly relieved although Christy was sure Josh had never admitted to his involvement with her. Josh would be... What would Josh be? Christy found herself quite uncaring. Josh had been a figment of her imagination. Ashe was a real man. He carried the aura of authority and achievement. He commanded respect at the same time treating every man, woman and child on the station the way they wanted to be treated, with kindness and fair-mindedness. They could come to him and tell them of their difficulties and he would listen. Christy had witnessed that many times. Small wonder for such a vast station things ran smoothly.

Gemma waited until after dinner to launch her missile, her sense of triumph barely veiled. Perhaps she wasn't aware Ashe already knew what she was about to tell him? She was leaving tomorrow—her father was flying in to collect her—but before she left she was going to create a few ripples for one Christy Parker who sat at the dinner table in an outrageously pretty dress, her face bedecked with soft smiles.

Christy looked radiant, Gemma thought; jealousy sending icy cold shivers down her back. What new thing had happened to make

Christy look so lit from within? She was an impostor, a fraud. She was on Augusta under false pretences. Surely Nic didn't know about her past? Unthinkable she would have kept it to herself or allow this impostor to look after her children. "What I've been trying to figure out," Gemma began as soon as she could, filled all day with a violent urge to get her seething emotions off her chest, "is how you put it over on us all, Christy?"

"What are you getting at, Gemma?" Ashe asked coolly.

Gemma took a long swallow of her delicious wine.

"I really didn't want to upset you with this, Ashe, but did you know Christy here who looks like a model for a medieval angel has been leading a double life?"

Ashe leaned back in his high-backed carver chair, brilliant eyes hooded. "Out with it. I wondered how long it would take you."

For a moment Gemma went quiet. "Wh-a-a-t?" No one but no one could look as formidable as Ashe when he so chose.

He leaned forward, snapped his fingers. "You don't have to be a genius to work it out. You and your mother have devoted some time and effort to checking Christy out. That's it, isn't it?''

''Only because we care for you, Ashe,'' Gemma said, putting out a hand to him, great earnestness in her eyes. ''It looks very much to us as if Christy has planned all this.'' Her voice sounded shocked and saddened.

''What is *this?*'' Christy spoke for the first time, studying the other young woman who faced her across the gleaming mahogany table.

Gemma's whole body language changed. She leaned forward like she wanted to surge across the table, eyes flashing her primitive emotions. ''I'm absolutely certain Nic and Brendan know nothing about your past. Let alone Ashe.''

''You're suggesting Christy has a criminal record?'' Ashe asked in a voice though deceptively soft might have given anyone else pause.

''Not a criminal record, no,'' Gemma continued, unable to leave well alone. ''But she's been enormously deceitful. I don't really like saying this—''

''Then why are you?'' Ashe asked very smoothly, brows like black wings above his brilliant eyes.

Gemma dragged her eyes away from Christy to stare at him. ''I know how much you value the truth, Ashe. Christy Parker has come here under false pretences. I know you'll find this hard to believe. I did, so did Mother, but Christy was seriously involved with—'' Gemma looked down, bit her lip ''—with Callista's husband,'' she finished in hushed tones.

''Is that it?'' Ashe drawled, almost casually.

''My God, isn't it enough?'' Gemma stared at him as though he had suddenly gone mad. ''No one knew her at the wedding. We've asked all around. Finally we got some information from one of Josh's colleagues. He said Josh's former girlfriend was very beautiful. He'd only seen her once. A blonde Josh had been keeping all to himself. No one really got to meet her but he said he thought it was serious. Very serious.''

Ashe's mouth twisted wryly. ''That was before he met and fell crazily in love with Callista and her millions.''

''I mean it's so weird!'' Gemma felt like her bombshell had failed to detonate. ''What was she doing at the wedding? What is she doing here? Who is she? She's not one of us.''

For an instant Christy, catching Ashe's darkening expression, thought he was about to verbally lash out. ''Gemma,'' she intervened quickly, her voice surprisingly kind, ''Ashe knows all this.''

''He can't.'' Gemma tried to swallow the hard lump in her throat. Couldn't.

''He does. What I don't see is that it's any of your business. What did you hope to achieve by saying all this? Josh isn't a bigamist. It's over between us. He married the woman he loves.''

''No, it's not as simple as that,'' Gemma protested, visibly quivering. ''There's a trick in it somewhere. I bet Nic doesn't know about your involvement with Josh.''

''I wonder you haven't gone ahead and faxed her,'' Ashe said.

''I don't know where they are,'' Gemma admitted artlessly, as though she felt thwarted she couldn't contact them with her news.

''Listen to me, Gemma,'' Ashe turned fully on her, speaking firmly. ''If you really want to remain a friend, and I don't want to lose your family's friendship, perhaps you could start by not interfering in *my* family's affairs.''

Gemma blinked hard—"But it's so unlike you, Ashe. So extraordinary. This girl has totally bedazzled you. Why I bet she's no different from your mother."

Gemma certainly knew how to bring all good feeling to a halt.

Ashe fixed her with brilliant angry eyes. "Okay, here you are. Your protestations of trying to help won't work. We both know why you're doing this."

"But you *don't!*" Gemma all but shouted, strangely pale. "I love you, Ashe. I'd make you a really fine wife. What you don't need is someone like *her!*" She threw a vengeful hand across the table, almost upsetting her tall-stemmed wineglass. "How could a woman like that devote herself to station life? She knows nothing about it. All she can do is ride."

"I was born and reared on a farm, you know," Christy pointed out mildly, when she was feeling the bliss of the day was quite spoiled.

"Why don't you walk away from this, Gemma?" Ashe sounded a warning. "You don't love me. You've made an art form out of wanting what you can't have."

At that Gemma jumped up, in her fury making her substantial, carved mahogany chair rock. "She's not good enough for you, Ashe. She'll be just like your mother and *disappear!*"

Ashe inhaled on a rasp. He stood up, too, a formidable figure, brow furrowed. "No more, Gemma. I mean it."

Gemma could see the hopelessness of it all in his face. Ashe had never loved her but he wanted this girl. "Wait until Callista hears of her treachery," she cried. "We all grew up together. We care about one another. That can't be lost. *She's* the alien in our midst. She'll bring you nothing but sorrow."

And then she was gone. Racing from the dining room, her slim body hunched awkwardly as though fending off blows.

"Oh my God!" Christy breathed, resting her head on her hand. "I feel so sorry for her."

But Ashe's eyes were hard and cold. "Don't bother. That was just a performance. She's out to cause as much trouble as she can."

"So what are we going to do?"

"I thought we'd done it." He suddenly snapped and banged the table. "As far as I'm concerned we're engaged as from today. I

know you hated to cause Gemma any embarrassment—you're too tender-hearted—but you
could have worn your ring tonight.''

''I'm not so cruel. I didn't want that. We
agreed. She does love you, Ashe.''

''Like you loved Deakin?'' he shot off, then
shook his head as if to clear it. ''No, no. I
didn't mean that.''

''I think you did,'' Christy told him quietly.
''I'm as upset you are, Ashe, but no one is
going to make me feel guilty. That includes
you. I thought I was in love with Josh. I see
now that was no more than window-dressing.
Josh showed himself in his true colours by going after Callista. He always wanted money.
Now he's got it. I'm hoping Callista is woman
enough to make him toe the line.''

CHAPTER SEVEN

JOSH had picked up considerably since his indisposition. In fact he had never looked better. Boyishly good-looking, tanned from a tropical sun, eyes sparkling, shining sun-bleached floppy hair, stylishly dressed in casual designer gear, well mannered as always, and attentive to his bride who to Christy's concerned eye looked washed out and drained of energy. Not the radiant young woman of her wedding day at all. Though obviously it hadn't been a honeymoon idyll with Josh taking ill.

"You're so good to have us, Ashe," Callista was saying in her soft tones, looking up at her cousin and smiling with gratitude. "I didn't think I could take going back to the city so soon. And Christy!" Callista just couldn't believe it. The exquisite blonde from her wedding day waiting for them at the homestead. She might have been warned!

"How are you, Callista. Lovely to see you again," Christy responded in her friendly fashion. "Josh!" She nodded her head in his di-

231

rection, not feeling in the least awkward or embarrassed. Ashe's ring hung between her breasts. In a few months' time she would marry him. Tonight after the announcement their relationship would be perfectly open. It would be such a relief. She had hated the deceptions however necessary.

"It was so nice of you to offer to look after Nic's children." Callista was still radiating powerful surprise. "She must think a lot of you?" Instinct warned Callista to be very wary of Christy. There was a story there she hadn't heard. It was obvious, too, Christy had endeared herself to the entire household. Ashe, Lonnie, the children, and the rest of the staff all appeared to look to her as though she were, heaven forbid, Mrs. Ashe McKinnon. Of course any woman could take her cousin Ashe away, Callista had been prepared for that, but she'd been hoping for someone sensible and moderately attractive who would be happy to share Ashe with his family. Someone like Gemma. This young woman was too beautiful, too sexy, too under-awed by everything. Worse, she would take up all of Ashe's attention.

Studying his wife's expression, which near revealed her somewhat bleak ruminations, Josh said solicitously, "Darling, why don't you go up to the room and rest awhile?" He was ready to steer her by the elbow. "I think Callista caught the bug, as well," he explained to the others, bending to kiss Callista's temple tenderly. "She hasn't been terribly well either." His excellent spirits were no more than a blind. He had been just as shocked as his wife to see Christy installed at the homestead, which was so big and so grand it pointed up all the things he had missed in his own life. Callista and her splendid arrogant cousin, who Josh knew, had no time for him.

Josh made to move, unsettled at the way McKinnon was looking at Callista, his expression concerned. "Are you sure you don't need to see a doctor, Callista?"

"Of course not." Callista struggled to sound brighter. "It's all the travelling. Josh has taken the most marvellous care of me. I've never felt so pampered. But I will go and lie down if you don't mind. I want to feel rested before Mummy and Nic and Brendan arrive. Augusta is the best place in the world to feel safe."

Safe? That was disturbing. The word took Christy by surprise. She'd been hoping Callista would feel perfectly safe with her husband who appeared to be making every effort to cosset her. Maybe it would turn out well after all.

Callista and Josh, arms entwined, retreated to the comfort and privacy of the spacious bedroom that had been prepared for them while Christy continued with her plan to take the children for a drive. Metta was to come along, the most delightful of guides. Metta knew all about the desert's wild fruits and flowers and their medicinal uses, the best lagoons and water channels. She could name all the birds, big and small. She knew the nests for the parrots, the cockatoos and owls and the secretive pelicans. Perhaps the most captivating aspect of her company, Metta had a great fund of stories from the Dreamtime, myths that identified her own tribal past. Ancestral creators had made the world shaping every natural feature of the earth. Metta had a magical story for everything; wind, rain, sun, fire, the blazing rocks that were such a desert feature, the birds and the desert animals. Christy found herself as fascinated as the children by these stories.

Their journeys around Augusta had established themselves as happy and educational times.

Ashe walked to the Jeep with them, taking Christy aside for a moment while Metta and the children made themselves comfortable in the vehicle.

"Callista didn't look too well, did she?" he asked, his eyes beneath the wide brim of the akubra sharply keen and a touch worried.

"Some people aren't good travellers," Christy soothed. "She'll probably feel better after a rest. She was very surprised to see me."

Ashe laughed. "Her husband wasn't crazy about it either. Doesn't he look amazingly healthy after so recent a bout of sickness?"

"That he does," Christy agreed wryly. "Maybe it wasn't as bad as they said. The sickness could have carried over to Callista." She turned up her face to him. "We have to tell them the truth, Ashe. The sooner the better. I want to come out into the open."

"Do you think I don't? What is the truth anyway? You had a brief romance with Deakin. It was all over by the time Callista came into the picture. Naturally we couldn't go into all that at the wedding. It was hardly the time. I hate white lies as much as you but they can act as a social lubricant.''

''Of course. But it *will* come out eventually.'' Christy gave a troubled sigh.

Ashe studied her, gratified Deakin's arrival hadn't disturbed her equilibrium. Finally it was over. ''As far as explanations go, leave it to me. I intend to announce our engagement right after dinner. You want that, don't you?''

''We've made a serious commitment to each other, Ashe.''

''We did and nothing is going to disrupt it.''

''No.'' She looked up at him very seriously. Her identification with Ashe was very new but not fragile. It was strong. She didn't doubt him. Her body trusted him. So did her mind. But there were other people with opinions to weigh in. ''I don't know how everyone else is going to take the news.''

''Frankly, I don't care.'' He tipped her chin, pressing a thumbprint into the shallow cleft, then dropped a kiss on her mouth that set her heart drumming. The first time ever he had done such a thing with the children and Metta looking on in apparent delight. ''Anyway, you're a woman with a lot of grit.'' There was challenge in his black eyes.

"You think it's going to be tested?"

"Well a few things have to be reconciled. Callista won't be full of joy about her husband's knowing you and not saying."

"She could scarcely catch up with it all at the wedding," Christy offered wryly. "For that matter, no one really got around to explaining why I was there."

"*I* invited you," Ashe said, with magnificent carelessness. "I didn't have much choice other than to invent a reason to avoid unnecessary hurt. They can accept it, not try to sort it out. I invited you to the wedding. We met when I was in Brisbane for a cattleman's conference some time back. You were doing P.R. work at the hotel. We fell in love at first sight. Such is my nature I couldn't get you out of my mind. I had to have you."

"Do you?" Little pulses began to beat inside her, like fiery little prongs.

"You think I like living with you and not having you?" he said. "When the house is dark and you're all curled up in bed... I could have walked down the verandah anytime."

"But you played it safe?" Her voice was very soft and husky. Didn't he know she yearned for him?

He laughed briefly. "It would have been the very time Kit would have woken up with a nightmare."

"So the children have been my little chaperones?" She couldn't have withstood him otherwise.

"Plus the fact I gave you my word you'd be perfectly safe. Now of course we're engaged," he added, his eyes sparkling with dangerous thoughts. "And the kids are going home. Who couldn't fall in love with you, Christy?"

Whenever he looked at her like that the world was reduced to just him. Christy flushed, a surge of bright blood colouring her skin. "And with you," she whispered, the seed of hope inside her beginning to flourish.

The children were bouncing up and down in the Jeep, unable to contain their excitement and gasping through their laughter.

"We saw you kissing Christy," they cried in unison, flinging themselves forward and waving their hands.

"So you noticed?" Ashe tweaked one of Katey's shiny curls.

"It was great!" Katey grinned broadly. "We're going to tell Mummy and Daddy."

"Whoaa, there!" Ashe gripped their small hands, leaning into the Jeep. "Now listen, guys, it's a secret until tomorrow," he said slowly. "Can I have your promise?" He looked very seriously into their wide eyes.

"*Our* secret?" Kit asked, sounding like that was very important.

"Our secret. You bet!" Ashe confirmed, keeping a hand on each of them.

"Then we'll keep it locked up," Katey promised solemnly, turning to her little brother. "Won't we, Kit?"

Kit was concentrating hard on this. "It's luv-ly you two kissing," he said finally. "It means you're going to love one another for-ever and ever."

Christy felt her heart swell with such emotion she wanted to cry. Instead she reached in and stroked Kit's warm satin cheek.

It was Ashe who answered for both of them, using a tone of voice so tender, so intense, Christy realised with deep emotion she had never heard him use that exact tone of voice before. "Until the end of the world," he said.

The children were ecstatic when they first caught sight of their parents, waving through the porthole. The Cessna charter flight taxied down the runway and came to a halt a turning distance from the main hangar. Callista, still looking pinched, had remained at the house with Josh in attendance but Christy accompanied Ashe and the children down to the landing strip in good time to see the Cessna bearing Callista's mother, Mercedes, and the children's parents fly in.

There were lots of hugs and kisses, a few tears from Nicole who had missed her beloved children even as she and Brendan were enjoying a holiday that had turned out to be so piercingly sweet, so full of love and warmth, it had been as Brendan said almost daily, ''a second honeymoon.'' All the old fire was back in their relationship and Nicole had begun to look at life in a new way. Nothing could minimize the loss of her child but she had a wonderful husband and two adorable children to share her life. She realised she was blessed. Mercedes was having trouble locating her luggage. She had brought rather a lot of it for a short stay. Ashe had her driven up to the house by one of the staff. Mercedes was very anxious to see her daughter for any number of reasons. The rest of them tumbled into the Jeep.

"We can't thank you enough, Christy, for looking after the children so beautifully," Nicole said, smiling comfortably. This was on the way back to the homestead, Nicole and Brendan having listened to the children's excited chatter and all the wonderful things they had done.

"It was a pleasure." Christy returned the smile. "I loved their company."

"We're real friends." Kit, on his mother's knee, looked at Christy owlishly, letting her know he wasn't about to say anything about their secret.

"That's true," Christy laughed.

"And we've got presents," Nicole told them in a happy voice.

"My goodness have we got presents!" Brendan gave a theatrical sigh. "I know because I had to buy another suitcase to bring them home."

"And Callista and Josh are up at the house?" Nicole asked of Christy. "It really is a shame Josh became ill."

"He's over it now," Ashe said smoothly, just barely turning his head. "Callista is the one I'm concerned about. She doesn't look at all well."

"It must have been catching." Nicole's carefree expression became serious. "Anyway we're all here now to cheer her up."

"Does anyone need cheering up when they're barely home from their honeymoon?" Ashe asked dryly. "I have to say you two look terrific."

"It was a marvellous, relaxed time." Nicole blushed delightfully. "I desperately needed it. I'm so grateful to you both for making it happen. Now I'm home with my beautiful children." Nicole hugged Kit to her.

"I can't wait to see what you've got us, Mummy," Katey said. "You and Daddy must see all our beautiful paintings."

"Paintings, oh my!" Nicole ruffled her daughter's hair.

"I think you'll be very pleasantly surprised," Christy promised. "Both the children have shown real promise."

Brendan turned back to stare at them. "I was pretty good at one time."

"You're still pretty good," Nicole said, nodding her head proudly, then nodding it again. "The children have inherited their talent from you. Did you know, children, Daddy once had a showing at a gallery?"

"Why did he stop?" Katey asked.

"Because I was responsible for my family," Brendan explained. "I'm an architect, sweetheart. That's my profession. It satisfied my artistic soul."

Hours later Christy was taking care with her dressing when a knock came at her door. She went to it hoping it was Ashe, instead Mercedes, looking very regal, stood outside the door, her generous figure clothed in her favourite dark blue silk, her trademark South Sea pearls around her neck.

"May I come in, my dear?" She sounded crisply decisive as though she intended to come in regardless of what Christy had to say.

"Why certainly, Mrs. McKinnon." Christy stood back, thinking the time had come to fully explain her presence at Callista's wedding reception. "Won't you sit down?" She indicated the deepest, most comfortable chair.

"I prefer to stand, my dear, if you don't mind," Mercedes said, addressing the chair. "I won't beat about the bush. It's not my way, but I had a most upsetting phone call from Gemma Millner-Hill."

Christy felt the heat in her face. ''She seems unable to mind her own business.''

''But it's my business, my dear.'' Mercedes changed her mind and lowered her statuesque figure into the armchair. Her face composed itself into censure and shock. ''Indeed it appears that you and Josh, my daughter's husband, knew one another *very well*. I find it absolutely extraordinary it was never mentioned. Would you mind enlightening me?''

Christy shrugged, taking a chair opposite. ''I deeply regret the deception, Mrs. McKinnon, but it was scarcely the best time to mention the fact at the wedding, especially as Josh hadn't mentioned it beforehand. The fact is Josh and I had a brief relationship that came to nothing. We weren't suited. It was over before Callista came on the scene.''

Mercedes levelled her with a highly dubious stare. ''My dear, I'm not happy with that explanation.''

''What explanation would make you happy, Mrs. McKinnon?'' Christy asked. ''I mean no impertinence. The last thing I want to do is upset you or Callista.''

''That's true, is it?'' Mercedes couldn't keep the anxiety out of her voice.

"I'm being absolutely honest when I say that."

"Why did Ashe invite you here?" Mercedes asked, wanting more clarification. "I thought Ashe told me everything."

"Maybe you could ask him," Christy suggested pleasantly.

"One doesn't…" Mercedes hesitated.

"Put Ashe on the carpet?" Christy cut her short.

"I don't press him about his affairs," Mercedes returned very briskly.

"I'm absolutely certain he's going to tell you." Christy tried to reassure her. "What is it that makes you fearful? Can't you tell me?"

The aggrieved look on Mercedes' face disappeared. "Callista desperately needs this marriage," she said. "She's deeply in love with Josh. Gemma gave me to understand you were planning some sort of upset?"

"Surely not for Callista. I promise you, Mrs. McKinnon, I've moved on in my life. Josh Deakin has no place in it," Christy said with great earnestness, looking directly into Mercedes' eyes.

"But surely, dear, he was close to you for a time?"

"He was, but people break up every day. I imagine Josh in not telling Callista only wished not to upset her."

"Perhaps Josh still cares for you?" The cloud redescended on Mercedes' fine forehead. "You're a beautiful girl. You have a very charming manner. Can either of you put your feelings so easily behind you?"

"Speaking for myself, most definitely. I don't regret knowing Josh. But I assure you I have no romantic interest in him now. It's all over, if it ever existed. Gemma was clearly out to make trouble. She didn't like my being here. She didn't like the fact Ashe and I have become close."

"Close?" Mercedes cried, as though something awful had happened. "But my dear, there's hardly been time."

"Time enough." Christy smiled gently. "I'm sorry you had to find out from Gemma that Josh and I were once friends, Mrs. McKinnon. It's apparent she put the worst possible slant on things."

"But you *were* going to speak about it, my dear," Mercedes challenged, regarding Christy with some worry.

Christy nodded. "I wanted to desperately but the time was never right. Neither of us can pretend it isn't a delicate matter."

"That's so." Mercedes shook her head ruefully. "I suppose this is one of these times when one shouldn't delve too deeply?"

Indeed it was, Christy thought wryly. She couldn't endure too much of not being forthright.

"Now why do I believe you?" Mercedes sighed. "I don't know you at all and I've known Gemma all her life."

"Do you think it might be because Gemma is going through a difficult time. She had this big affair with Ashe but it's all taken place in her own mind. One wouldn't have to be a detective to find her aim was to discredit me."

Mercedes made a jerky movement of the hand. "But Ashe hasn't given us a hint about any romance with you. You *are* telling me there's something between you?"

"I'd like you to hear it from Ashe, Mrs. McKinnon," Christy said. "He's family. He has a great deal of love for you and Callista."

On that they were in agreement—Mercedes allowed herself a smile. "He's been absolutely marvellous to us. A rock, in good times and bad. Ah well, my dear—'' she made a sudden move to get up ''—I do hope I haven't upset you in any way but I thought I simply had to get things straight. I never thought for one moment Gemma was capable of being so vindictive but then jealousy does do strange things to people.''

Both women walked to the door, Christy deciding she could risk a question of her own. ''Mrs. McKinnon, do you mind if I ask you a question? It's not idle curiosity. It's important to me.''

Mercedes nodded her stately head. ''Go ahead, my dear.''

''Your sister-in-law, Eve, Ashe's mother, you must have known her well?''

Mercedes was so surprised by the question for a minute she didn't say anything. ''I did,'' she admitted, a little cautiously. ''Such an enchanting creature but not suited to station life at all. They should never have married but they were both terribly in love.''

''Her leaving had a profound effect on Ashe.''

''Of course it did!'' Mercedes agreed immediately. ''Ashe idolized his father. Looked up to him, respected him. Charles was such a fine man, but Ashe loved his mother in a different way. She was like sunshine. She always kept Ashe happy and laughing. She was a very warm, affectionate person, very demonstrative. Charles wasn't like that. He'd been reared to believe a man should act in a certain way with discipline and authority. He didn't clown around, if you know what I mean. Eve was full of fun. Charles was enormously proud of Ashe. He was very much the son and heir, but they didn't have the marvellous easy relationship that existed between mother and son."

Christy felt she had learned something entirely unexpected. "So how did she come to leave him and at such a tender age?"

"She was pregnant, my dear," Mercedes informed her bluntly. "If you didn't know it before you know it now. A mad moment when Charles was away. Of course Duane fell in love with her on sight. I shouldn't excuse him but in some ways he was as much a victim of circumstance as Eve. For one thing, when he visited Augusta—a business trip—he never expected to meet anyone like Eve. In the end he took her away but Charles was never going to hand over his son. Eve was the guilty party and Charles was a very powerful and influential man. There was no question she would get custody of Ashe. She thought she would be able to see him often but Ashe himself made that impossible. Anger used to spill from him in those days and it grew and grew. He blamed his mother entirely for the break-up of the marriage.''

''It's a tragic story,'' Christy said faintly.

''For Charles and Ashe it was very, very hard. Eve keeps hoping some day Ashe will forgive her. He has a half brother you know.''

''Yes, Ashe told me.'' Christy looked into Mercedes' fine eyes.

''Then he trusts you, my dear. That counts for a lot. Ashe doesn't speak about his mother to anyone. I've seen Eve many times over the years when I'm overseas. She's still beautiful. Duane has made her happy. She leads a full life in her own sophisticated milieu, but the memory of her firstborn still haunts her.

''The irony is, Duane Junior is not unlike Ashe in appearance. Both have their mother's eyes, various expressions, the physical grace. But Duane is a softer, easier, boyish version. He doesn't have Ashe's inbuilt air of command or the sometimes daunting aura Ashe can slip into so easily. Duane wants to meet

his half brother so much I shouldn't be surprised if one of these days he simply turns up
on Augusta. His father doesn't want him to
follow up the connection but it's a different
story with Eve. Ah well, lots of changes go on
in life." Mercedes sighed. "Now I really must
go. By the way—" she half turned, for the first
time pleasure in her expression "—that's an
extremely pretty dress. I love the ultra-
feminine look but I could never wear it even
as a girl. Too tall, too big-boned."

"You're a very striking woman, Mrs.
McKinnon," Christy said. It was perfectly
true.

"Mercedes, dear." Mercedes was inclined
to think now what Christy needed was accep-
tance.

"That's very sweet of you." Christy smiled.

"If you ask me," Mercedes said propheti-
cally, "Ashe has a surprise to spring on us all
tonight."

All through the dinner party cum family re-
union Josh Deakin held on to his equilibrium
for dear life. He couldn't blow it now. He had
a wife who to his surprise he didn't mind at
all. In fact he had more or less made the com-

mitment to make a go of his marriage but how his heart, or his body, he wasn't sure which, cried out for Christy. He had to brace himself constantly for the sight of her sitting across the gleaming expanse of the long formal dining table.

It was all so spectacular! The table was laid with a sumptuous gold-and-cream cloth, beautiful gold-and-white china, solid silver flatware, flanked by crystal wineglasses that must have cost a mint. Two very tall vases held a profusion of yellow- and apricot-coloured roses. Solid silver candlesticks with cupids cavorting around the base marched down the table. It was terribly impressive, all linked to who the McKinnons were and what they were.

McKinnon presided at the head of the table, insufferably handsome with a striking profile. Josh coveted his jacket. Italian of course, a very fine black-and-white check. He was very much master of a great historic station leading the conversation that sparkled and eddied around him. He hadn't thought the cattle baron could be so witty, so relaxed and charming. McKinnon at the helm of his adoring family. That very much included Callista. She doted on "darling Ashe." A serious and sour note.

He would always have McKinnon looking over his shoulder and he'd better get used to it.

While Josh thought himself unobserved, Ashe's dark eyes missed nothing. He could see Callista's husband with a startling clarity; read his mind. Deakin couldn't hide his sense of envy and jealousy. He'd even caught Deakin staring at his jacket. No doubt wondering about the label and how much it had cost as if one piece of information wouldn't reveal the other. Most of all—as host he had to remind himself this would pass—he had counted the number of times Deakin's eyes, subtle and sly, had been drawn irresistibly to Christy. As if any man's eyes wouldn't be, he was dazzled himself, but with Deakin it was different. He and Christy had a past history. He was certain on Christy's part it was just that, but Deakin appeared to be one of those men who didn't like to let go.

On this special night Christy was wearing one of her wonderfully pretty dresses, a kaleidoscope of sea greens and violets, the V neckline plunged down her creamy skin to the rose-tinged cleft. She had beautiful breasts, the skin like the silken petals of a flower. He wanted no other man's eyes on them. Certainly not Deakin's. Nic and Brendan were being nice to him, but he knew, like himself, it was more for Callista's sake than any genuine feeling of friendliness. That was reserved for Christy.

It gave him great pleasure to know Christy got on famously with his family. Even Mercedes appeared to have taken a shine to her, but not Callista, Ashe noticed, and sympathised. Callista was feeling threatened. Perhaps she had already begun to notice how often her new husband's eyes strayed in Christy's direction. It would have that disquietening effect on her. Callista deserved her happiness. His only great regret was she had fallen in love with the wrong man. Reinforcing his own theory love made a person helpless. Love—he knew that also led to betrayal.

He wanted to snatch Christy up and sweep her away. Above all make love to her in the sparkling moonlight. The sensation of it ran up and down his body like a flame, but he was resigned to getting through dinner without actually giving Deakin a punch on the nose.

Sometime later Ashe judged it time to call his guests' attention. He tapped his wineglass and they all fell quiet, leaning forward so they could look at him directly. ''With all my family around me, and I welcome Josh to our number—'' he was forced to incline his head toward Josh ''—I have some news that I know you've long been waiting for. I've finally chosen my beautiful bride. I know I've rushed her terribly, indeed I haven't given her a moment to change her mind, but I knew the moment I laid eyes on her I'd never let her go. Of course I'm speaking about Christine.'' He turned to Christy, picking up her hand and carrying it to his lips. ''Christy has made me very proud and happy by consenting to marry me. This dinner party with us all together marks the official start of our engagement.''

While the others looked on in rapt surprise, he withdrew the magnificent ring he had retrieved from Christy from his inner breast pocked and slipped it on her slender finger, her nails lacquered a soft pearly pink.

My God, the family emeralds! Mercedes thought, knowing the full story behind how they were acquired and Eve's defection with the necklace.

Everyone seemed to jump up at once, exclaiming their delight and congratulations. All except Callista who sat cheeks flushed, eyes glittery, trying desperately to get a handle on it all.

And Josh. He sat stunned, the most dreadful sense of loss mixed with anger and envy bearing down on him like an express train. How could this have happened? Christy loved him. He had expected her to keep a place in her heart for him forever. Yet here was McKinnon looking exultant as though his every plan, his every strategy, had been fulfilled. Christy was so absolutely heartbreakingly beautiful it sliced through him like a knife. Her face was illuminated by emotional radiance. She was hugged and kissed, drawn into the family. Of a sudden, a sick fury pulsed out of Josh like blood from a cut artery. He couldn't absorb the shock. It was a wound, so raw, so open, it momentarily overcame him. His hand gripped his wineglass tighter, tighter—he couldn't let go— it fragmented into three large pieces, a shard piercing the skin, causing blood to flow.

''I don't believe it!'' he gestured a little crazily, the words bubbling up from his tight throat.

The focus of attention shifted entirely to him. No one could escape his words or his expression.

"Josh, please," Christy appealed in quivering fright, unaware of the hard tension in Ashe. "Look what you've done to your hand!" She said it to deflect Ashe more than anything, but it turned out badly.

Now neither of them could escape their involvement. Neither had a chance to recover. The familiarity with which Christy had spoken Josh's name, the expression on her face, the concern and dismay misinterpreted seemed to speak volumes.

"You know him, don't you?" Callista cried out with a spurt of rage. She made no attempt to go to her husband; to help him staunch the flow of blood. "You know *my husband?*"

Here it comes, Christy thought.

Ashe looked at his cousin, a warning in his eyes. "Don't be so tragic about it, Callista. It's not some terrible thing though you should have been told."

"By whom?"

"*You* never told me." Callista turned her wrath on Christy, a sorry sight as her normal good manners disintegrated.

"I'm not sure *I* had to, Callista," Christy appealed, as upset in her way as was Callista.

"We dated for a while but it was all over when he fell in love with you."

Callista's hurt and anger was terrible to see. "He *loved* you," she said, looking utterly convinced. "You're just the sort of woman to drive men crazy."

Mercedes tried desperately to quiet her daughter by putting her arms around her. "Darling girl, I'm afraid you're overreacting."

But Callista shook her mother off with some violence, her breathing coming like a hiss. "All along I've been worried about you. Little things continually nagging at me. Little things I was trying to forget."

"Perhaps you didn't hear what I've just said, Callista?" Ashe's voice was abnormally quiet. "Christy and I have just announced our engagement. I really can't have you making things difficult for her. Neither do I want to spoil our night."

Angry as she was Callista had little choice but to back off. "I'm sorry, Ashe. So sorry, but I can't seem to get things right." She closed her eyes as though she was about to step off a cliff. Then of a sudden she jumped, lightning-quick. "I can't help feeling in marrying this girl—'' with one finger she pointed to Christy ''—you *can't* have known her long enough—you might be doing something you'll regret.'' She completely ignored the fact she only had a short courtship herself, hating Christy simply because she once had a relationship with her husband which in turn gave her a stark and narrow perspective.

Ashe sat back in his chair, frowning. This was supposed to be a night of celebration, ruined by Callista and her no-good husband. Nevertheless he tried hard to temper his words because he knew Callista was at some crisis point. ''Callista, I know you're not well,'' he said with a forgiving air. ''But please stop now. This isn't a matter for you to interfere in. In marrying Christy, I'm doing exactly what I want.''

Shocked and humiliated, her bravado exhausted, Callista abandoned herself to floods of tears. She pushed back her chair, overwhelmed by the enormity of what she had just said. ''Sorry, Ashe. Sorry. I'm profoundly sorry.'' She dashed from the room, not pausing for a moment to look back at her husband of fragile character.

"Lord save us!" Mercedes intoned, never having sat through such an experience. Ashe had been goodness itself to her and Callista. Now this!

"Callista really isn't herself," she apologised. "I'd best go to her." Mercedes followed much less dramatically in the path of her daughter, suddenly struck by the thought Callista could be pregnant. Everything seemed to fuse together. The sickness, the queasiness, the tears and emotional outburst.

"Are you going to go to your wife?" Ashe demanded of Josh, his patience at an end. Josh was busy pressing Brendan's clean white handkerchief to his cut hand.

That was quite a performance of Callista's, he thought. He didn't know she had it in her, but reacted nervously as they all stared at him. "She mightn't want me."

"Right now, I'm not surprised. What the hell were you trying to do?" Ashe's nostrils almost exhaled smoke.

Nicole and Brendan sat uncomfortable and dismayed as Josh tried to pull himself together, knowing above all he had to vindicate himself or he might be standing out on the highway, bags packed. "Your announcement was such a shock to me. That's all."

"The understatement of the year." Ashe's lean handsome face looked contemptuous. "Tell me, what are you planning on next? Are you going to stay with Callista, do you think?"

Josh flinched at the sarcasm. Upstairs Mercedes and Callista would be clamouring for his blood. He longed for the simplicity of his honeymoon when Callista adored him— how things were becoming complex. "I must make Callista believe Christy means absolutely nothing to me," he said finally, creating such disgust in Christy she burst out.

"You miserable…"

"Moron?" Ashe offered as Christy didn't permit herself the next word. It was the real Josh unmasked.

"So, are you going to go to your wife?" Ashe repeated, springing up from his chair, angry and imposing in every way. Disgust pressed down on him as he looked at Josh's good-looking but weak face. "What you should have said was *you* mean nothing to Christy. Or can't you admit that even to yourself? Whatever you do, don't make the mistake of interfering in my affairs. Nobody offers insult to Christy. She's my financée and in a short time she'll be my wife. If you want peace and quiet in your life, remember that.''

Josh could have smashed his head against the table so intense was his frustration. McKinnon's wife! What a dream run. So Christy had emerged the victor after all. Christy, the mistress of all this! It was incredible and he had brought it all about. Nevertheless he had to appeal to her. She was the only one who wasn't looking at him with open censure and disgust. ''I guess I've made a fool of myself,'' he said, trying to resurrect his charming self-deprecating smile.

''Here, here!'' Brendan seconded briefly.

''I guess you have, Josh,'' Christy told him gently, ''but it's nothing new. The only thing that can save you is, Callista really does love you. I suggest you go and make your peace with her. I can't feel angry with you. I have to take a lot of the blame myself, but without you I would never have met Ashe.''

A statement that increased Josh's grief. He rose to his feet feeling very much the outsider.

''Do you want someone to take a look at that hand?'' Ashe asked abruptly, just barely remembering Josh was his guest.

"It doesn't need stitching." Brendan settled the question by shaking his head. "The bleeding made it look worse than it really is. If you come with me, Josh, I'll get some antiseptic and some bandages from the first-aid room."

"I say, that's very kind of you." Josh smiled gratefully. He really needed to get away from McKinnon. The man thoroughly unnerved him.

"Better Callista than me," Nicole observed after Josh and Brendan had gone. "He's so charming on the surface."

"The surface precisely," Ashe said.

"I regret I couldn't tell you the exact position with Josh and me," Christy said, looking apologetically into Nicole's eyes. "The timing was desperately wrong."

"Yes, I can see that," Nicole acknowledged, beginning to understand the very tricky situation. "So you did know him well?"

Christy nodded her gleaming gold head, not looking at Ashe's darkly brooding figure. She could feel his anger and condemnation. It pierced her like a knife. "He let me down badly. I gatecrashed the wedding reception with the intention of giving him a good fright. Nothing more. Ashe saved me. Hard as it is to believe now, Josh's decision to marry Callista hit me for six. But it was all an illusion.''

"It happens,'' Nicole nodded.

"Well,'' Christy grimaced, "I thought it was real at the time.''

"Deakin could be delicately referred to as an opportunist,'' Ashe observed harshly. "I sensed that from the beginning, but I knew Callista would run over us all with a steam-roller to marry him. She loves him, if that's relevant to happiness?'' he added too bitterly, his upset at events and his mother's betrayal stored in his bones.

"I certainly think it is,'' Christy said bravely, unable to keep the deep hurt out of her voice.

"So do I.'' Sympathetically, Nicole reached over to cover Christy's hand. "Don't let their outbursts upset your night. It's clear to me Ashe needs you, Christy.'' To forget his childhood, Nicole thought but never dared to speak aloud. "I couldn't be happier for you both. Ashe has waited a long time to find his true love. Now he has her in you, Christy. I know we're going to be the greatest friends.''

*   *   *

Though they all tried hard after that, Josh and Callista between them had wrecked the evening. It wasn't until a good hour later that Ashe and Christy were finally alone. Both of them knew in their bones they were due for a row. Their first. It had been a while coming. Ashe, a passionate man for all his hard-won control, couldn't modify the terrible tension in his gut. He hoped and prayed he wouldn't say anything he would regret, but dammit all this was supposed to be the celebration of his and Christy's engagement, yet a forgettable character like Deakin had had the power to wreck it.

Now Christy stood within his study so beautiful, so feminine, she was transcendant. Her green eyes sparking with little gold currents, revealed her knowledge of the intensity in him. God, the very last thing he ever wanted was for her to be afraid of him. Yet he could see her trembling and anxious when all he wanted to do was take her in his arms. Instead he walked past her and locked the cedar door, so thick and heavy it would muffle all sound.

"Hell, what an evening," he groaned. "Come and take a chair."

"I thought I was to be put on the mat?" Christy answered, feeling herself under tremendous strain.

"Don't be ridiculous," he answered far too shortly, but his control was collapsing. Not so his desire for her, which was amounting to obsession.

"*Is* it ridiculous?" she challenged, remaining where she was on the Persian rug. The light from the bronze chandelier like a thousand candles illuminated her beautiful hair. "This morning I felt wanted, needed, above all *understood.*"

"So what's changed?" He didn't know, couldn't know, how he appeared to her, his eyes as black as night, his expression broodingly forbidding as he fought the very dazzle of her.

"Josh and your cousin between them have shattered all that," Christy said, her voice ragged with disappointment and tight nerves. "They've shattered your trust in me. Don't deny it. I can see it in your face. You're a hard man, Ashe. Without love in your life you could become ruthless."

He grimaced with high impatience. "I don't see that at all. What I did see was your concern and dismay' at your ex-lover's cutting his hand.'' He watched her guilty flush, saw her lace her fingers.

Christy could feel herself lose all composure. ''Now *you're* being ridiculous. I didn't give a damn about Josh cutting his hand. It was you I was worried about. You and your temper.''

That rocked him. No one had ever accused him of having a bad temper. ''Have you ever *seen* it?'' he demanded, outraged she should look at it that way.

''I know it is in you,'' she retaliated, at the same time wondering where all this was going. ''I'm seeing it now. Where does your sweet cousin Callista get off abusing me? I've done nothing wrong. The only mistake I made was falling for Josh's superficial charm. And he does have it whether you like it or not.''

That sent a brilliant flash of jealousy through him. ''Listen to yourself,'' he invited, his tone deeply ironic. ''Josh has charm. Charm! My God, you should despise the man. *I* do. With good reason. He married Callista for her money. What he fully intended was to retain you for a lover.''

Christy stamped her foot in rage and frustration. "How dare you!" Her rage was also directed at herself. Of course she despised Josh. "And I'm supposed to be your fiancée," she cried scathingly. In her over-emotional state, she began to pull at her glorious ring. It came easily. She threw it at him, knowing with his superb reflexes he would catch it. "I'm not interested in your blasted marriage contract," she told him fiercely. "I want a man who trusts me enough *not* to have one. You don't. Your supposed trust in me is paper-thin."

He couldn't stop himself retaliating. "Your actions tonight didn't help any. We all saw your concern, which you now say was for *me*. Callista didn't see it that way either."

"That's right, take Callista's part." Her voice resounded with hurt. "Your precious family. God, I'd always be an outsider. Your wounds have never healed, Ashe. Do you know that?"

"Maybe badly wounded hearts never heal," he responded grimly. "In your place I would have told Deakin off."

Her voice choked. "That's unfair, but then you are unfair. It was hardly the time. Or the place. Do you think I didn't want to? You invited them here, not me. I would never have had them. Let them work out their own lives. And just fancy Callista talking about *our* short relationship. She couldn't wait to rush Josh to the altar. If you're jealous—though God knows you don't know enough about caring, certainly not for *me*—there's no need to be. I can't bear to say this one more time. Josh means absolutely nothing to me.''

''Then why don't you tell *him* that?'' An answering anger ripped through him. A terror of losing her. He could feel pain everywhere, to the tips of his fingers. He wanted happiness. He wanted her. He couldn't let it all crumble. He wouldn't. She was going nowhere. It crossed his mind he was going mad. Mad with love for her.

Like a man driven, he went to her and pulled her into his arms. Her beautiful blond hair streamed over his arm, her face averted. Yet he kissed her, not sparing his hard passion.

He might have held a statue. Her arms hung at her sides, never seeking to embrace him. Summoning his strength, he let her go.

She was very pale where she had been flushed before. Her iridescent eyes were filled with tears.

Shocked at his own brutality he fell back against the massive desk. ''I'm sorry, Christy,'' he apologised from the bottom of his heart. ''I didn't mean—''

''You *did* mean,'' she cut him off. ''You've wanted to hurt me and you have.''

Every word was like a nail in him. ''No, please, no.'' He made a grab for her hands, but she pulled them away. ''Christy, please listen…''

''Unlock the door, Ashe,'' she said, her voice cold. ''We've both said things I know we'll regret.''

''Don't let them stay with you,'' he begged. His pulses were pounding, his nerves jangled. He didn't want to let her go but to force her was unthinkable. Whenever he had kissed her before her response had been exquisite. He couldn't bear for her to fear him. But it seemed she did.

Outside the moon was magic. Inside the light had gone out.

Ashe moved to the door and turned the heavy key. As she moved close he put his arm around her waist. ''Do you really hate me so much?''

"No," she told him, with bent head, "I love you, Ashe. God knows why."

The homestead was very quiet. So quiet Christy could hear the far-off howling of a dingo. Such a weird primeval sound. It made the hairs on the back of her neck stand up. The wild dingos she had seen, especially in the hill country, were magnificent animals, not all of them gold, some nearly pure white, highly intelligent but killers by nature. Their instinct was to hunt. She knew they were a menace to the herd. They were even a menace to humans. Savage attacks were not unknown. The dingo continued his mournful song while Christy padded fretfully round her bedroom, unable to settle. She'd thought Callista's outburst had upset her but it was as nothing to her row with Ashe. And this was supposed to be her engagement night! It had started out so brilliantly only to be shot down in flames.

"I think I can trust you with a little secret, Christy," Mercedes had confided. "It might take some of the upset away and help you understand. Callista thinks she's pregnant."

Christy privately thought if it turned out Callista wasn't pregnant it might be better if she quit while she was ahead. It was evident to Christy a man like Josh—he wasn't a real man at all—would make Callista suffer. Still, Callista wanted him. If anyone said a bad word about Josh she would have exploded like a firecracker. It was their life. They had to work it out.

As for her and Ashe? He almost defeated her. She knew Callista's outburst had upset him, but then, it had upset her.

Sleep was a long way off. She was much too overwrought. Her end of the house was lonely with the children down with their parents. She had never stayed in a house before that boasted twelve bedrooms, all of double size. Would she ever be mistress of all this? After tonight it seemed doubtful. Callista and Josh would be tucked up in bed by now. Perhaps reconciled? No one knew better than Josh how to spin a good cover story. He'd had so much practice.

Mercedes had gone off a little tipsy. A double celebration. It was only to be expected Mercedes would adore a grandchild whether Josh was the father or not. At least Josh didn't have jug ears or any noticeable physical imperfections. The McKinnon blood would help the child. What interested Christy was when had Callista fallen pregnant if indeed she were? Sweet little Callista might have had a few strategies of her own. Maybe forward planning ran in the family?

Eventually churning with regret and forces too strong for her to handle Christy went in search of her impossible fiancé. She had been startled at her own hostility, her mind turning over every hurtful remark to the extent it made her head throb. Ashe could be such a formidable man. She had never known anyone whose arrogant features could so marvellously depict contempt.

Her slippered footsteps were inaudible through the house. She knew he hadn't yet retired. No matter his pre-dawn start, Ashe never went to bed early, thriving on a handful of hours sleep. She could see the brilliant chink of light was still beneath his study door. The rest of the very large homestead was in soft gloom. The sound of her own breathing was startling, so was the swish of her satin robe.

Keep moving or retreat. Especially after that confrontation. She loved him so much but the man was so complicated. She crept a little further towards the light. She stood motionless, listening to her own heartbeat. The grandfather clock further down broke into a series of chimes that nearly made her jump out of her skin. In fact she gave a stifled cry.

Midnight. The witching hour.

Suddenly she began to wonder what she was doing, robbed of confidence in her position in Ashe's life. On this night of nights she had wanted to be feted, caressed, adored. She wanted him to take her to his bed. Passionately desired it, but as the woman he loved, not some damned possession. Christy turned, making up her mind to flee, let tempers cool down, only Ashe emerged from the study, moving so fantastically fast he caught her up before she had gone a few yards.

"So you've come back to me?" His warm breath was scented with fine spirit. Whisky, brandy, she didn't know. Maybe he'd been drinking away his anger.

She spun in his arms, the agitation of the night fuel to the fire. "You've got me in a trap."

"No one gets out of my traps either," he said, "not alive!" He laughed beneath his breath then, like a pirate, swept her up into his arms. "It's been too long. I've tried to be your shining knight but God, I want you too much."

The electric charge through her blood was fantastic. She struggled though he was much too strong. "Put me down, Ashe." She trembled over her words. "It's you and your history. You're heartless." Glorious. Unforgettable.

"If you think that you're as screwed up as I am," he drawled. "Why don't you just lie quiet?"

"Ashe...please..." she begged, all helplessness, disorder, long hair trailing, the sash of her satin robe undone.

"You're not leaving me tonight. Not when you came back of your own free will. In fact you're not leaving me at all. Think of that. You and me together. Every night of our lives."

All manner of emotion charged through her, raising her to an unprecedented pitch. Excitement, passion, residual sadness. This man could break her heart.

"Hush." He dipped his dark head to her. "It would be too, too risky to disturb the household. I just might tell them all to leave." He threw her a brilliant smile, taking the rear staircase at an impetuous rush, holding her as though she weighed no more than Katey. At the top, not even out of breath, he went soundlessly down the hallway that led to his private master suite.

A massive wave somewhere between panic and excitement broke over Christy. Inside his massive bedroom with its baronial four-poster Ashe threw her onto the heavy brocade quilt, dark gold in colour. The springs were so good Christy bounced. He put out a hand to trace the curved outline of her mouth. ''That mouth of yours,'' he exclaimed, low-voiced.

Christy's pulses were soaring. Dangerous hormones flooded her blood. Whatever it was he had real power over her—no question.

''Move over,'' he said.

''Is this an attempt to seduce me?'' She was flushed and defiant, the defiance gossamer-thin.

''No attempt.'' He bent over her with powerful languorous grace. ''If you didn't *want* it, it would be an entirely different matter.''

''You're so sure.''

''Of you, yes.''

Silently she made room for him, lost in her own desperate need. It was overwhelming to be in his bed, his nearness, his male fragrance and strength an invincible force. How she loved the beauty of the eyes that sought hers. He was marvellous. Brilliant. Difficult. She loved him so much all memory of life before him seemed to dissolve.

Christy closed her eyes the moment his hand contoured her breast gently but commandingly, pushing the soft satin aside so he could see her; caress the smooth creamy skin. His thumb circling and circling the tightly furled nipple, his ministrations leaving her trembling in his arms.

''You're so beautiful,'' he murmured. ''I'm so sorry for before. Forgive me.''

''I'm sorry, too.'' How easy it was to say it.

''Of course I trust you. It was jealousy speaking. I've been out of my mind wanting to do this since the night you walked into the reception. So audacious, so sexy.''

Her back arched in rapture as he pressed his mouth over hers, kissed and kissed her again, with such sensuality she felt her very bones dissolve. His tongue moved against hers, slid around her teeth. Her robe had fallen away, now his hands moved over her body, tracing, exploring, learning it, now it was his. The stimulation was so enormous he had to cradle her. Christy moaned aloud as he found the valley between her slender legs, his fingers emitting a deep hunger but such tenderness it was almost a reverence.

"You're like silk," he muttered. "I want you so badly the need is almost splitting me open. Yet I want this to last forever." He bent his dark head, his lips brushing warmly, ardently against her throat.

She knew she whispered something, his name, an endearment, but never the forbidden words I love you, though she was leaving herself wide open to the most intimate of caresses. Eventually he levered his lean powerful body over her. He still wore his clothes, his shirt unbuttoned to the waist, but she was barely draped in her nightdress, her breasts and thighs exposed to his touch and his sight. The conjunction of their bodies made her heart contract. Two flames melted into one. She could feel the driving force of his sex. He radiated an exquisite fire, a passion that was sublime. When her heart was almost bursting, and she was unable to contain the need that palpated within her like great wings, he rose from the bed, stripping his splendid darkly tanned body of its clothes.

"My Christine. My angel."

To Christy's immense joy it sounded like a meltdown of all remaining doubt. His vibrant voice was deep, half crooning to her. His brilliant dark eyes were no longer veiled enigmas; they revealed the deep emotions that were in him. Emotions as vast and encompassing as his desert fortress. He was breathing deeply as he covered her, yet Christy heard very distinctly what he said.

"You know, don't you, my darling, this is no more than *love*."

EPILOGUE

Four months later.
The McKinnon-Parker wedding ceremony and
reception—Augusta Downs Station
South West Queensland

SOME ten minutes before the bride was due to make her appearance in the beautiful old ballroom that had been turned into a flower-decked temple, a tall slender woman walked quietly down the centre aisle and slipped into the front pew. To many of the guests she was not only extremely glamorous but also vaguely familiar. Others knew *exactly* who she was. The former Eve Elizabeth McKinnon. In her mid-fifties Eve was still stunning, her willowy figure dressed in the height of fashion, her beautiful blond hair twisted into an updated chignon. A small turquoise feather and rose creation adorned her head, the chic headpiece colour matched to her elegant two-piece suit and the satin shoes on her feet.

She appeared not to care or even notice that everyone in the ballroom was staring. Eve smiled down the line of seated guests in the front pew. All McKinnons—all extremely sensitive to her presence. Her former sister-in-law, Mercedes, who had never fully blamed her, sat beside her for comfort and support. She desperately needed it. She owed a lot to Mercedes who looked splendid in a light blue outfit with a big blue hat banded with curled silver ribbon. Further down sat Mercedes' daughter, Callista. Clearly Callista was pregnant but wearing a cleverly cut yellow silk dress with an eye-catching orchid-trimmed cream hat. Her attractive well-dressed husband was beside her. Among the others Eve noted was a very good-looking young woman with startling blue eyes who was regarding her with a hint of gentle encouragement. Could it be Nicole? Eve's mind turned back twenty years and more. Of course, little Nicole. Her husband was one of Ashe's attendants.

Eve focused her gaze with intensity, willing herself to take command of her emotions, which was not easy. Her vulnerability was immense. Her firstborn stood before the satin-draped altar table. At first meeting with him less than twenty-four hours before she had been out of control with emotion, all her hidden grief rising to the surface like a giant gusher, reflecting the great sadness that lay beneath her poised facade. Always she had carried her memories. Carried the guilt for the great wrong she had done her husband, the damage to her son. But her son had survived, to become a magnificent figure in his formal wedding clothes.

Ashe was flanked by his attendants, his best man, a life-long friend and his two grooms. The youngest of them was Eve's other son, Duane. Duane had been thrilled out of his mind his elder half brother had not only wanted to meet him but suggested he might like to act as his wedding attendant. Why not? In meeting Ashe, Duane was finding his own family. Eve had told herself countless times she couldn't afford to become over-wrought but the scene in front of her threatened to overwhelm her. She knew this room. Many a gala function had been held there. Eve had to fumble in her bag for a lace-edged handkerchief.

Ashe and Duane. Her sons. They had both inherited her dark eyes and other physical features she could rejoice in. She pushed back

into the ribbon-decked pew, straightening her
shoulders. Her husband hadn't wanted her to
make this long journey. He saw nothing to be
gained from trying to relive her past. Only she
felt this was her golden chance to repair some
of the terrible damage she had done. The loss
of contact with her firstborn was the central
tragedy of her life. Eve acknowledged it almost every day though she had a husband and
son who loved her.

"Why deliver yourself up to them?" her
husband had demanded, deeply concerned she
could be received badly. But he wouldn't go
with her. He, too, felt the guilts and burdens
of the past.

Mercedes, acutely aware of the crackling
static of Eve's emotions, put out a sympathetic
hand. Eve had won herself a place at Ashe's
wedding but Mercedes knew just how much
courage it had taken for Eve to get herself
here. Many of the McKinnon clan were still
hostile to Eve though social etiquette demanded they try to keep it well hidden. Of
course none of this would have happened without Christy. Christy was the architect of it all;
the one who had worked the miracle of getting
mother and son together. It hadn't happened

easily, Ashe had been very difficult to sway, but Christy had never given up. And of course Ashe loved her. That's what settled it. Christy had told Ashe many times the past had to be reconciled before they could look to their future. Christy had become a powerful influence in Ashe's life. Mercedes was happy about that, certain Christy over time would become part of the McKinnon family legend.

At the rear of the ballroom while the wedding guests waited in eager anticipation, Christy took her proud father's right arm. The wonderful entrance music, an emotional force, pealed out to uplift her to the skies. She smiled at her proud father as the bridal procession began its slow stately walk up the ruby-carpeted aisle. Her bridesmaids in extraordinarily beautiful and imaginative gowns, headdresses on their upswept hair, walked in pairs. There were four: Montana, Suzanne, Philippa and Elise. Slender and glowing as irises in purple, rose-pink, royal-blue and emerald-green silk taffeta. Behind them heralding the bride were her two little friends, Christopher and Katey, page boy and flower girl; Katey dressed in white and cream silk with little appliqués of gold, Kit absolutely adorable in a cream suit with a cream-and-gold brocade waistcoat and white cravat. Their perfection increased Christy's emotional reaction.

She was the central figure. The bride.

Every head turned as she moved into the room. Little ripples of pleasure broke out spontaneously all around the large room. Her friend, Kelly, an honoured guest, had designed all the gowns and the children's outfits. Christy didn't know it then but her truly glorious wedding gown was destined to put the young designer friend on the fashion map. Of magnolia duchesse satin, organza and exquisite gold lace, the bodice was a stunning duchesse satin strapless corset over a fairy-tale billowing skirt with floating panels of gold lace that matched the short flaring veil. The strapless gown showed to advantage the magnificent emerald-diamond necklace she wore around her throat. The same emeralds and diamonds winked at her ears. But what was infinitely more beautiful than her gown and precious gems was the radiance within her. It streamed out of her like rays of sun. Everything about her spoke of her great love and joy. It was this exultation that moved the assembled wedding guests profoundly and reminded them all marriages, in all faiths, had been destined to be a sacrament.

At the altar Ashe stood before the bishop who had baptised him and who was now smiling on him most benignly. Ashe wasn't just waiting for his bride, he was holding his heart in his two hands. His heart was hers. Although he had been told many times he looked superbly in control on this day of days, his throat was thick with emotion. For so long he had become accustomed to suppressing emotion but his beloved Christy had changed all that. She had altered his life in every conceivable fashion and taught him a whole new way of being. Now his heart soared in anticipation of his first sight of her in her bridal finery. He had dreamed of it but today was reality.

She was there! This was a single moment in time he knew he would carry with him all his life. It was all he could do not to seize her in his arms there and then and kiss every inch of her loveliness. He could see his desire reflected in her beautiful sparkling eyes.

What is love? he had once asked, his mind clouded over with doubts. He knew the answer to that now. Ashe turned to his bride, openly adoring her. She took his breath. His so-called strategies had been no more than a last-ditch pathetic attempt to keep his heart tightly closed. It had cracked when his mother had left him. Now his mother and his half brother had re-entered his life. Again, thanks to his serene, compassionate Christy, she had caused it all to happen.

Christy. All the beauty in the world!

''My handsome prince,'' she whispered joyfully to him.

My queen. He would have died for her.

He knew it might take him a little while to fully express his great love for her; for him to really take his mother back into his life, not all of the old barriers had dissolved, but he knew with great certainty Christy would carry his children and the last word on earth he would whisper would be her beloved name.

MILLS & BOON® PUBLISH EIGHT LARGE PRINT TITLES A MONTH. THESE ARE THE EIGHT TITLES FOR NOVEMBER 2002

———————— ❧ ————————

THE BRIDAL BARGAIN
Emma Darcy

THE TYCOON'S VIRGIN
Penny Jordan

TO MARRY McCLOUD
Carole Mortimer

MISTRESS OF LA RIOJA
Sharon Kendrick

STRATEGY FOR MARRIAGE
Margaret Way

THE TYCOON'S TAKEOVER
Liz Fielding

THE HONEYMOON PRIZE
Jessica Hart

HER FORBIDDEN BRIDEGROOM
Susan Fox

MILLS & BOON®